In the 22nd century, Mother Earth is dying . . .

Humanity's last hope is a lushly green, oxygen-rich planet twenty-two light-years away. Visionary pilgrim Devon Adair leads the first expedition to this new Earth. But a malfunction strands Devon and her crew far from their destination of New Pacifica. Now, their only hope is an impossible journey thousands of miles across an unknown and hostile planet . . .

And they won't be alone.

EARTH 2

Puzzle

The journey continues . . .

And don't miss the fantastic debut novel . . .

EARTH 2

Available from Ace Books

Earth 2 Novels from Ace Books

EARTH 2
PUZZLE

EARTH™ 2

P U Z Z L E

A NOVEL BY

SEAN DALTON

Based on the Universal Television and
Amblin Entertainment television series *Earth 2*
created by: Billy Ray
and Michael Duggan & Carol Flint & Mark Levin

ACE BOOKS, NEW YORK

Earth 2: Puzzle, a novel by Sean Dalton, based on the Universal Television and Amblin Entertainment television series *Earth 2* created by: Billy Ray and Michael Duggan & Carol Flint & Mark Levin.

This book is an Ace original edition, and has never been previously published.

EARTH 2: PUZZLE

An Ace Book / published by arrangement with MCA Publishing Rights, a Division of MCA, Inc.

PRINTING HISTORY
Ace edition / February 1995

ISBN: 0-441-00148-3

ACE®
Ace Books are published by The Berkley Publishing Group, 200 Madison Avenue, New York, NY 10016.
ACE and the "A" design are trademarks belonging to Charter Communications, Inc.

PRINTED IN THE UNITED STATES OF AMERICA

10 9 8 7 6 5 4 3 2 1

EARTH!™ 2

PUZZLE

Chapter 1

· · · · ● ● ●

The mid-morning sun hung heavy above the horizon, a
sullen copper ball behind a hazy curtain of dust and heat.

Rolling desert plains stretched out on all sides, wide and
endless, a sea of dusty brown scrub. Here and there a
solitary tree stood, leaves coated with dust, its bark tattered
from being chewed by animals.

The heat was an oven, radiating as much from the
hard-packed ground as from the sky. Riding the red ATV
ahead of the travelers trudging slowly along, Devon Adair
lowered the map a moment and gnawed worriedly at her lip.
For the last hour she'd been thinking they might be lost.
Now she was almost positive.

She debated with herself, wondering if she should notify
the others, but she was in charge, and getting the colonists
to their destination was her responsibility. She wasn't ready

to admit a mistake yet, especially not until she understood how it could have happened.

She leaned over the robot head, which had been attached to the ATV today to drive for her, and checked its electronic compass. They had drifted off course again.

Small wonder they weren't turning up any of the landmarks on her geological surveys.

Devon frowned. "Zero!" she said sharply to the robotic head doing the driving for her. "Correct back onto course. This is the third time this morning you've veered off."

"Sorry," Zero said meekly. "Will correct."

The ATV slowly moved left in a diagonal line, its treads lurching over a small gully and nearly tossing her off the seat. She clutched the handbar and hung on grimly until the ATV was stable again.

"Very cute," she said through her teeth and squinted up at the sky. Her skin felt as though it were drying into jerky. She pulled off her hat to shake the sweat from her brown hair. Although the motion of the ATV created a slight breeze in her face, no wind stirred to provide relief for the travelers following her. She glanced back to make sure she wasn't choking them with dust. Bess, nearly hidden beneath a broad-brimmed hat, gave her a little wave.

Their pilot, Alonzo Solace, had gone ahead, scouting in the DuneRail to locate a campsite for their midday stop. In this heat, they'd been traveling until noon, resting until the sun dropped to the horizon, then traveling on until bedtime. It was Devon's goal to make the river by midday, then establish a campsite where they could rest for a few days, make repairs, hunt for food, and enjoy the luxury of unlimited baths.

At the rear of their small column the huge TransRover lumbered along slowly. Devon squinted at the sunlight reflecting blindingly off its solar panels. Inside the glass cab she could see John Danziger's silhouette, with two shorter figures sitting beside him. Danziger and his daughter, True, were probably boring little Uly to death, but at least Devon could be sure her son was protected somewhat from the heat and choking dust.

On the maps, this open terrain looked ideal for walking, unlike the thick forests ahead. But they hadn't counted on the oppressive heat or the powdery dust. The stuff fogged everywhere. Even at this slow speed, the vehicles threw up clouds of it, and every trudging footstep from those walking stirred up more. If the wind blew at all, it always seemed to come at their backs, thus sending the dust back over them. Everyone's clothes were coated white. Julia had suggested people tie wet cloths over their noses and mouths for protection. Devon's mask had long since dried out. She uncapped her canteen now, allowing herself a single swallow, then splashed a small amount of water on her face and throat. The momentary coolness felt marvelous. For a moment she imagined the river ahead and how it would feel to plunge her entire body into the water.

The image, however, only made her feel hotter. With the ATV stopped, there was no breeze at all. Devon scanned the group, making a swift, periodic count of heads to be certain no one had strayed. She had a fear of losing someone to the unknown dangers of this planet. Since they'd crash-landed, so many things had seemed to go wrong. As leader of this expedition, it was up to Devon to get these people safely to their colony site of New Pacifica. With sufficient vehicles, they could have cut months off their travel time. But there was no point wishing for the contents of those missing cargo pods. As Bess was always saying, they had a lot to be thankful for. The space station they'd left had been a so-called perfect environment, and it had nearly killed Uly.

Devon was glad to be here, thankful to be here, even if unexpected problems kept landing in her lap.

At the moment her primary concern was finding the river. Their water supplies were running low, and Devon had counted on it to replenish the tanks on the TransRover.

So where were the landmarks she expected to find?

Fanning herself with the map, she flipped on the ATV's sensor array and wiped a powdery coating of dust off the screen. Her hard-copy map had been drawn by Yale, utilizing probe information and the government's orbital surveys of the planet. The map was beautifully done, but Yale had been hampered by the vast amount of uncharted terrain. Many distances were off base, and Devon kept having to refigure the bearings. Zero's erratic driving was only making things harder.

So where the hell was the mountain range they should have reached by now? The probe had indicated it as a continental divide. A river supposedly flowed along its eastern flank. She squinted at the horizon and estimated visibility to be about forty klicks despite the dust and general haziness. No mountain range in sight in any direction. The scanners were sweeping. No mountains registered within their range either.

A soft chirp sounded over her gear, and she adjusted her headset swiftly to be sure the call was on a private channel for her reception only.

Alonzo's lean, handsome face grinned at her via the vid inset.

"Hi," she said. "How's it going out there?"

"I'm about ten klicks ahead of you, running northwest," the pilot said. "Want me to continue on or come back in?"

"What have you found?"

"Nada, querida." Even over the gear's static, his voice

4

was warm and charming. The vid image scattered momentarily, then reformed. "Are you sure Yale can draw a map?"

A soft beep came from the scanners, and she frowned. "Hang on a moment."

She leaned over the dash eagerly, but all the screen showed was a cloudy sweep of life forms moving ahead. They were roughly on Alonzo's heading. Devon sighed in disappointment.

They'd seen several herds of antelope-like creatures already since they reached these arid plains. The animals were timid and harmless.

"You find what you're looking for?" Alonzo asked.

"Nope." She switched off her sensors in disgust. "You're going to run into a herd of something. Might as well turn back and join us. I think it's time to have a meeting."

"Better you than me," Alonzo said without much sympathy. "I'll swing back, maybe check a few other things on the way."

He switched off before Devon could protest. Grimacing, she set her gear back to general mode.

She glanced over her shoulder at the people trudging along and felt fresh guilt. "Some kind of leader you turned out to be," she muttered aloud.

Although she'd already done a visual scan, she checked everyone's homing devices over her gear. All present and accounted for. So how long was she going to delay admitting they had a problem? The river at the base of the mountains was the only water source within a hundred miles marked on her map.

The group was unlikely to panic. They'd proven their mettle a dozen times over. If they hadn't been tough, they'd never have ventured out here in the first place. She had to get over trying to protect them.

5

Still putting off the confrontation, Devon instead checked in with her son. "Uly? You there?"

His response was slow in coming. "Sure, Mom."

"Doing okay?" she asked. Although Uly's health had continued to improve dramatically since their arrival, a ten-year habit of constant worrying over him had become too ingrained to shake easily. She intended to leave nothing to chance, and took nothing for granted.

"Yeah, I'm fine," he said impatiently. "Just hot."

"We're all hot."

"Yeah, and I'm thirsty too."

Devon's frown deepened. *Did you bring your son across all these parsecs to a frontier world just to kill him of thirst?* asked a tiny, mocking voice inside her.

She brushed the voice away. She wasn't beaten yet. If they tightened the water rations further, they could last for days yet.

"Mom?" Uly said. "Uh, could I ride with you for a while? I need to ask you something."

She had to grin to herself. He *was* getting tired of the Danzigers' company. "I thought you wanted to see the scenery way up there on top."

"Yeah, but—"

"Breaking in," John Danziger said over her gear. "You've slowed way down. Are we stopping or are you waiting for everyone to catch up?"

Devon frowned. "We're stopping."

"Problem?" he asked.

"Maybe."

"If we're stopping," Uly said, "can I have a drink?"

"Okay," she said. "We'll all take a little break here."

"Right here?" Danziger asked. "Why not crest that next ridge, maybe catch the breeze a little?"

Devon glanced ahead. Her ATV was crawling along a shallow dip between two ridges. Aside from the steady buzz of insects in the weeds, there was no other sign of life. Beyond the engine noise of their vehicles, silent emptiness hung over the world.

"I think it's about equal," she said to Danziger. "Up on top of those rocks would be like a griddle. We're not stopping long. Somewhere along here is fine."

"You're the boss," Danziger said and got off the channel.

"Mom," Uly whined. "I need to tell you something."

"Later, okay? I'm busy right now. Ask Yale to give you and True some water. But keep it a small drink. We're still on rations."

"But—"

"Be sure you put on your mask before you get off the TransRover. I don't want you breathing dust."

"Yeah, Mom."

She knew that bored, impatient tone well. "Uly, I'm serious. If you don't keep it on, you're going to be back on your breathing apparatus, understand?"

"Mom!"

"I mean it," she said sternly.

"But True thinks I'm such a dork—"

"I don't care. True is different."

"But I don't have The Syndrome anymore!" Uly wailed.

Devon's temper started to slip, but she held it together. Uly had been a very sick child all his life. They both needed time to adjust to his recovery. Perhaps he was accepting it better than she was.

"Sure, you're fine now," she said with as much patience as she could muster. "But it's hotter than you think, and heat is dangerous. No running around. No exploring. Stay in the shade with Yale. It's about time for your lessons anyway."

He didn't answer her.

She frowned. "Uly?" she said sharply.

"Okay, okay," he said in a sullen voice.

Devon could hear True's voice saying something to him off gear. Devon switched off. She couldn't spend all day arguing with a ten-year-old child.

Tossing her map into the storage bin, she braked the ATV and switched her gear to general broadcast: "Heads up, everyone. Let's take a rest."

Behind her, the straggling line of dust-coated colonists slowly came to a halt. Coughing and talking among themselves, they removed their hats and fanned themselves or slapped dust from their clothing. Others flopped down on the hot ground without even bothering to create temporary shade for themselves. Devon watched worriedly.

The bright yellow DuneRail popped over the western ridge and came speeding down to her. Sunlight reflected brightly off its solar panels as Alonzo looped around her in a fancy maneuver and braked sharply in a cloud of dust. Grinning with the charm that had women in every space port dreaming of his return, he looked Devon over and raised one dark, handsome brow. "I thought maybe I'd better lend you my support."

"Thanks," she said wryly. "Got tired of the scenery?"

His dark eyes flickered, but his grin didn't fade. "Maybe. There's a big dust cloud to the south. See it?"

She looked to her left, but in this low place her view was cut off. She shook her head. "What is it?"

He shrugged. "Hard to say. Big though. On top of the ridges, you can see it. Might be worth checking into."

She leveled her gaze at him. "Right now we have more important things to worry about."

"Yeah, like being off course."

"Even if Zero's nav unit is malfunctioning, we should still be able to see the mountains," she said in frustration. "It can't be a simply case of course drift."

Alonzo raised his eyebrow again. "I've been piloting ships longer than you've been alive. Hand me that map you've been going by."

She dug it out of the storage bin and handed it to him. Alonzo bent his dark head over it, muttering to himself.

"Devon!" Morgan Martin said sharply, coming up. Normally neat as a pin from his boots to his ponytail, today Morgan looked as grubby and frazzled as everyone else. Sweat made tracks through the dust coating his face. "What's going on? Why have we stopped? The decision was to keep going until midday."

Devon opened her mouth to answer, but he swept on, unheeding. "And why here? There's not a scrap of shade anywhere. No wind in this canyon either."

"We're not in a canyon."

"We'll roast to death."

"Morgan, there's—"

"Speed, speed, speed, that's all you think about," he complained. "You mark off a certain designation of klicks to be covered for a day, and you by God push us all mercilessly to get there. I know why you stopped here. No sign of anything to hunt, no shade, no chance of catching a breeze at all. You don't want us to linger, do you? No, you want an uncomfortable campsite so we'll be willing to go on. But we can't keep marching in this heat. It'll kill us. Travel by night; rest by day. That was my suggestion."

"And a good one," she said, trying to break in.

"But now you've changed the procedure," he said, eyeing her suspiciously. "Why? A breakdown? Is something wrong with the solar panels?"

"Stop making this worse than it is," she said in exasperation. "It's a temporary stop, okay?"

Morgan frowned suspiciously. "Obviously. I keep asking you why, and you keep evading me."

"Maybe if you'd let her answer one question at a time, you'd get more answers," Alonzo said.

Devon glanced over at the others. They were all busy talking and gathering around the water tanks. She didn't want Morgan to be the sole hearer of bad news. "Zero's head is malfunctioning," she said, dodging the issue a little longer. "I keep getting a course drift, and I think it should be checked out."

Alonzo rolled his dark eyes her way and smirked, but she ignored him.

Morgan shook his head. "Oh, no. No way. Zero doesn't malfunction. You must have set the bearings incorrectly."

"Look," Devon began angrily. "I—"

"One way to settle this," Alonzo said, breaking in. Stepping around Devon, he boosted himself onto the seat of her ATV. "I'll take a little spin. Maybe check out that dust cloud. It's bigger than the one we're stirring up."

"Alonzo, it's not important now."

He met her eyes with his dark brown ones. "Maybe we'd better be very sure Zero's nav unit is okay. You read me?"

She nodded, understanding all too well.

Morgan frowned. "What does that mean? Alonzo—"

But the pilot was already roaring off with a cloud of dust and a jaunty wave.

Devon sighed, knowing that every time she delayed telling everyone the truth she made it harder for herself. She swung around and switched her gear to general broadcast mode.

"Everyone, check your canteens, but remember to stay tight with the water rations," she said. "Julia, any problems with dehydration?"

"No cases so far," the doctor replied. "Walman and Bess have a touch of heatstroke. Nothing serious, just a little shaky. The rest is a good idea. I'd like to rotate this pair among the vehicles when we start up again this evening."

"It's too early to stop for the day," Devon said with annoyance. "We haven't gone far enough."

Julia didn't trouble to answer. Without looking around, Devon could feel Morgan's disapproval at her shoulder. She remembered his scornful words: *You mark off a certain designation of klicks to be covered for a day, then you by God push us all mercilessly to get there.*

And if they didn't get to water, Devon reminded herself, they'd learn what "mercilessly" really meant.

She could feel the heat radiating off the hard-baked soil even through her boot soles.

Morgan wiped sweat from his face. He was still watching her closely. She forced herself to meet his gaze blandly, giving nothing of her worry away.

"I'm going to refill my canteen," he said finally. "This rationing is ridiculous. You persist in making things more difficult than they need be."

"It's called survival techniques," she said. They'd been over this argument before.

"Yes, and if things had been handled properly, we wouldn't be eating dust and suffering heatstroke," he said. "We could have our town set up by now. Things would be organized. We would be safe."

"There are no guarantees on a colony world," she told him.

He stared at her, not understanding, and shook his head.

11

"There should be. The entire expedition has been mis-handled from the very start. Even launching without authority—"

Her temper snapped. "You helped on that one, remember?"

"Yes, but I had no idea—"

"Just keep the details straight, Morgan."

"The details are that we were to land safely in New Pacifica. We were to have adequate supplies. We were not supposed to risk our lives out here in this godforsaken hellhole."

She'd heard it all before. From the moment they'd crashed. From the moment they'd discovered their cargo pods missing or raided. From the moment they'd encountered sentient life forms that supposedly didn't exist on this world. From the moment they'd started rationing food, water, and medicines. Morgan would always want someone to blame. He would always find something to complain about.

"Look," she said shortly, "we've alive, and we're together. My son is healthy for the first time in his life. I have a lot to be grateful for. How about you? Do you ever stop and count your blessings, or do you leave that to your wife?"

Morgan gave her a hard stare and walked off.

Turning her back to him, Devon looked for Danziger and gave him a wave. The mechanic waved back, then said something to his daughter. She nodded, grinning beneath the bill of her cap, and raced back to the TransRover.

"Danziger," Devon said impatiently on gear, "bring your tool kit."

"Check," Danziger replied. "Let me get some air set up first."

"Don't set up," she said impatiently. "We won't be here long."

As she spoke, she heard a low, distant rumble. It sounded like thunder. Feeling hope, she gazed up at the sky, but there were no clouds. Devon crammed her hat back on her head. Great. Now she was hearing things.

Everyone else clustered around the immense TransRover, where the water tanks were. She saw Bess Martin wave the doctor away and take charge of refilling canteens. Bess, at least, could be counted on to be fair, yet stick to the rationing amounts. Uly was sitting in the shade, trying to coax True's pet koba into playing with him. The animal, however, was too hot and sleepy to respond. Yale, his hands clasped at his back, stood stiffly to one side, not talking to anyone. He knew there was map trouble, and last night he'd offered to redo his work. But if the probe information was off, what good would that do?

Despite Devon's orders, Danziger and Baines set up the fans. Soon cooling sweeps of air crisscrossed the temporary site. Uly went over to stand in front of one, letting the air billow through his clothing. Even True stopped lubricating the TransRover's wheels and scooted out from beneath the vehicle to join Uly.

The majority of the dust cloud hanging with them lifted and blew away, driven off by Danziger's carefully engineered placement of the fans.

Devon opened the toolbox on the DuneRail and rummaged for a diagnostics scanner.

"Need some help?" Danziger said over her shoulder.

She jumped and turned around quickly to hide her startlement.

The mechanic stood there, looking even more rumpled than usual. A two-day growth of beard stubble covered his jawline. His eyes, calm and confident, regarded her without expression. A rifle was slung over his shoulder, and he carried his tool kit in one hand.

"Need some help?" he repeated. "You asked for the tool kit."

"I'm looking for the diagnostic," she told him. "Seen it?"

His expression shifted to that quizzical grimace she didn't like, and he pulled the scanner from his pocket. "Big or little problem?"

"Big," she muttered.

He frowned and stepped toward the DuneRail. "Alonzo been running it too fast again? He said the other day there might be a loose coupling in the feed from the panels."

"It's not the DuneRail."

"The ATV then." Danziger dropped the tool kit on the ground and rubbed his jaw. "Alonzo checking it for you?"

"Yes. Zero won't stay on course. There's a constant two-degree drift."

Danziger smiled in a way that didn't really reach his eyes. He was a taciturn, unhurried individual, independent from the others. Along with Alonzo, Walman, Magus, and Baines, Danziger was one of the ship's crew who had been supposed to drop the colonists off on G889 and return to the station. Being stranded with them hadn't been in his plans, but he wasn't a complainer. He was hired help, just the mechanic for the journey, and if and when they ever reached New Pacifica, he and his young daughter would be on the next ship heading back to the space station. Perhaps because of that, he tended to avoid the excitement of the others as they surveyed this new, wondrous planet that was theirs to conquer. When someone exclaimed over the scenery, Danziger looked as though he'd rather be reading a manual. While they all danced in the rain, Danziger burrowed off to check fluid levels in the TransRover. If they were lying around the camp fire at night, counting stars, Danziger could be heard pointing out the way home to True.

Home, Devon thought with a snort, thankful to be off the space station and the fast track of her old life. *This* was home. Their home. She stared into the distance, not as daunted now by the dry, forbidding aspect of these plains. More than enough room. More than enough resources. Unspoiled, untouched . . . theirs to shape. A chance to start over, to have a better life. Harder, sure, but definitely better. Especially once they found those damned mountains.

She realized, belatedly, that Danziger was saying something to her. Bringing herself back, she shook her head at him. "Sorry, what?"

"I said until Hotshot brings back the ATV, I can't check the nav unit for malfunctions. So why don't I go hunting in the meantime? We need some fresh food."

She shook her head. "We have to talk."

"Go ahead."

She glanced at her map. It was covered with scribbles and notations, plus a log of how many klicks they covered per day. The dark smudge of the mountains had been circled in red. She handed the map to Danziger, walked over to a small gully, and stood at its edge, kicking dust bleakly into its sandy bottom.

He followed her, lifting his hand to his left ear to switch off his gear. Devon did the same. There was no point in letting everyone eavesdrop on this conversation.

He held out the map, and she took it silently.

"I thought there was more going on here than a little dirt in Zero's nav unit," he said. "We're lost, aren't we?"

Her mouth twisted, but refusing to admit it wasn't going to solve the problem. "We are," she said at last. She stared

15

at the sky beyond the ridge and bit her lip. "The map's wrong," she said in a low voice.

"Sure," he said easily. "It almost always is."

"No, *really* wrong," she said.

"Look, if you're worried about the course drift, don't be. Everything's been erratic the last few days. Scanners need recalibrating, sensor arrays are off, nav units are starting to show drift. It might be the dust. It might be some kind of strong magnetic field in this general area."

Her head snapped around, and she looked at him with widened eyes. "Something Gaal's doing?"

Danziger shook his head. "Natural. The fluctuations are irregular. Anything manmade would be steady."

She let out her breath in relief. Their few encounters with Gaal had been unpleasant, to say the least. She was happy to avoid him if at all possible.

"Probably something in the mountains," Danziger went on. "Maybe ore with properties we don't understand or . . ." His voice trailed off and something changed in his eyes. "There are no mountains."

"No."

A muscle twitched in his jaw. "True noticed. She and Uly kept talking about them, asking me about visibility and how long until we should be able to see them. I wasn't paying much attention. Figured the distances were off, as usual."

"True was right. We should be able to see them. But we don't." Devon threw out her arms in a broad gesture. "There are no mountains!"

"Now, maybe there's—"

"Do you see any?"

"Well, down here in this dip it's—"

"But before, when we went over the last rise, did you see any?"

Little crinkles appeared at the corners of his eyes as he

squinted into the distance. "No. I told you I figured we weren't close enough."

"Well, we are. We should be two hours away from them. We should have been able to see them when we started this morning."

"So the map's off more than usual."

"No." She took it from him and with extremely precise movements folded it into a small square. "The map is dead wrong. I haven't found any identifiable landmarks since yesterday. I didn't worry too much. I checked and rechecked our bearings. We're where we're supposed to be. But the mountains aren't."

"So we'll—"

She gripped his sleeve hard, trying to make him understand. "Get this, okay? Visibility doesn't show them. The scanners don't show them. I sent Alonzo out ahead of us, and he hasn't found them either. We should have been able to see them days ago, but we haven't."

She slapped the map against her leg, stirring up dust. "I can't be *that* far off course. Not to miss a whole mountain range."

Danziger frowned uneasily. "You took a directional when we started this morning."

Devon nodded, telling herself she should be grateful for the mechanic's calmness. He hadn't blamed Yale and he hadn't blamed her. But irrationally she blamed herself.

"I set the compasses, took all the bearings, calibrated Zero's nav unit before and after I plugged him into the ATV's port. We've been on the move more than four hours, and I'm still not finding the landmarks."

Ahead of them another low rumble sounded. Devon glanced at the sky. Wherever the thunderclouds were, they weren't in sight.

Danziger rubbed the sweat from his face. "We were on course last night when we made camp. We can't be that far off already."

"I'm not so sure we were on course last night," she admitted. "Thinking back now, how can I be sure? How do I trace back to where the mistake started? Or was it my mistake? I've been careful. So has Alonzo." She held up the map in irritation and thumped it. "This is *wrong*."

"So have Yale redo it."

She sighed. "He's already offered, but what's the point? The data he's working from is unreliable. I don't know if someone in the survey team made a major error, or if it's a deliberate data change, but we can't trust it now. Which makes it useless."

"Don't overreact. The probes have been fairly accurate up till now."

"At least the major geological features matched up," she agreed. "Until now. But it's as though these mountains simply vanished."

"Maybe they did."

She eyed him, but he didn't look as though he were joking. Swallowing the temptation to be sarcastic, she said, "You're saying earthquake or some volcanic activity since the surveys were made? We'd see evidence of a seismic upheaval that large. Ash, hardening lava flow, something."

She gestured at the featureless land around them and shook her head. "Besides, all the information I've got on this area fails to indicate any tectonic plate instability—"

Danziger shrugged. "I'm no geologist. It was just a suggestion."

"In the meantime, theories don't get us any closer to our destination."

"Okay, so we're lost," he said. "But maybe not as much

as we think. We'll stay on this heading and keep going a few more days, until we can see the mountains."

"We don't have a few more days."

His brows snapped together, and he gave her a hard, intent look. "Explain."

She gestured back at the TransRover. "The water, John. The tanks are less than half full. If there's no mountains, chances are there's no river either. That's the only water source I have marked on this map until—"

"Let me see that again."

Taking it from her, he unfolded it swiftly and scanned it with a deepening frown. She reached over his arm and pointed at the next red circle she'd made on the map. "See?"

He whistled softly between his teeth and met her eyes. "We're in trouble all right."

He glanced over his shoulder at the colonists who were still standing in line to refill their canteens. "Damn," he said softly. "In this heat, they could lose all judgment. It's not like opening a faucet on the station, is it?"

"No," she agreed. "Reality is about to get tough."

His gaze narrowed. "Regrets?"

Her head snapped up. She wasn't going to admit anything, especially to a man who had no stake in this world. "None," she said. "I know we can extend our supplies if we tighten the rationing—"

"Not enough," he broke in. "Not if we have to go all the way to—"

"And what if the next water hole is bogus too?" she asked, finally voicing the fear that had been growing inside her all day.

He looked at her and didn't answer.

Around them, the brown, dry land stretched endlessly, a sea of weeds and dust. The sun beat hot on Devon's shoulders. Her shadow had shortened to mere inches. Soon the sun would be ahead of them, glaring into their faces with a wall of heat.

They could navigate by the sun and the stars. They could keep going. But without some landmarks they could trust, they might easily wander past a water source without ever knowing it. New Pacifica suddenly seemed farther from reach than ever.

In the distance Devon heard another long, muted rumble.

Danziger glanced at the sky. "Thunder?"

"No clouds." But she glanced up anyway. The sky was hazy and bright, like the bottom of a brass bowl. She squinted. "No rain."

He swore silently and turned away from the gully. He pulled at the back of his neck as though to ease tense muscles.

"I have to tell the others," she said.

All her worry lay in her voice. Devon wasn't afraid of responsibility. This expedition had been her idea. She'd selected G889 as a site for colonization. She'd pushed to obtain the permits. She'd sold the idea to others. But the prospect of leading these people to a potential death out here in the middle of nowhere filled her with trepidation.

Danziger looked at her over his shoulder. His eyes were very serious, as if he could read straight into her mind. "Yes," he said quietly. "I think you'd better tell them now."

"I can keep it quiet," she said. "Maybe we could go on a day longer. As you say, it could be only a distance lapse on the map. Or . . ."

She let her voice trail off.

Danziger's expression didn't lighten. "They deserve to know."

She nodded reluctantly, giving in to the prodding of her own conscience. "You're right. They do."

"I can tell them for you."

Her shoulders squared at once. "It's my job," she said tightly. "I'll do it."

His expression didn't change, but he seemed to approve. "I'll walk back with you."

Chapter 2

• • • • • • ● ●

A shout of laughter caught their attention. Uly was chasing True, squirting her with his pressurized canteen. She squirted him back, and with a bark of anger, Danziger ran toward the children.

"Cut it out!" he shouted. "True! Quit wasting water like that. Don't you know we have to be careful?"

True stopped playing and stood sullenly while he scolded her. Uly, who had started it all, edged away. Danziger caught his arm and lectured him too.

Devon hurried up. No one but her had the right to discipline her son. "All right," she broke in. "I'll handle this."

Danziger was still fuming. "Spoiled little—"

Devon pulled Uly's frail arm from his grasp. "I said I'll handle it."

The rumble came again, louder, closer.

"Hey!" shouted Bess from atop the TransRover. "Everyone, look! Did you ever see so many?"

Gripping Uly's hand, Devon turned with the others. A herd of shaggy gray creatures, four-legged and ungainly, with massive horned heads and bodies that seemed too large for their spindly legs, came streaming down the shallow canyon toward the colonists. Clouds of dust fogged everywhere. Red-eyed and snorting as though maddened, the creatures were running full-tilt, a thundering, galloping juggernaut that made the ground shake. Unlike the herds of other animals that veered in formation at the least appearance of anything startling, these animals came hurtling straight on.

And the colonists had stopped right in the bottom of the canyon, right in the animals' path.

For a moment Devon stood frozen by the sight, then she realized the danger.

"Everyone, break camp!" she shouted. "Move it, now, now, *now!*"

Morgan Martin hooted in derision. "They'll go around us, just like the goldbucks did. We can always scare them—"

"These aren't like the migratory herds we've encountered before," Devon argued. "Look at the way they're coming."

Standing apart from the others, Yale clasped his hands at his back and in the deep, expressionless voice that indicated he had switched to lecture mode, he said, "During the mid-nineteenth century, the western American states on Earth were covered with vast herds of bovine animals called buffalo. Migratory patterns of the animals indicated—"

"Forget that," Danziger snapped, shoving him. "Get moving. Take care of the kids."

"As many of you as can, get on the DuneRail," Devon ordered. "Everyone else, get on the TransRover." She pushed

Uly into Yale's arms and headed for the driver's seat while the others scurried to gather up their belongings.

"There's no time!" Danziger shouted. "Leave the equipment and run for the ridge."

"They're coming too fast!" Baines said fearfully. He glanced over his shoulder. "They're coming right at us. We'll all be crushed to death."

Zero lumbered forward. "I can stop them. I—"

"Zero, stop!" Devon ordered sharply. "We do not require your assistance. Climb that slope."

"But I can—"

"No, Zero. Comply with your instructions."

Reluctantly the robot turned and headed for the hillside.

Julia bumped into Devon. "Sorry. We've got to run."

"Come on!" Danziger shouted. "There isn't time to start up the equipment. Leave it!"

"He's right!" Devon said. She looked around for Uly and Yale. The Teacher was already running hand-in-hand with the boy, for the hillside.

Morgan helped Bess jump down off the TransRover and pushed her ahead of him as they ran. Danziger pulled True from the cab of the TransRover and gave her a shove.

She yelled something Devon couldn't hear over the rumble of a thousand hooves. True was screaming and trying to turn back, but Danziger shook her hard and made her go. Red-faced and crying, True yanked off her cap and ran, hair flying. Danziger and Walman waved at Devon to go, and the two men positioned themselves between the oncoming animals and the vehicles. Danziger lifted his rifle and fired.

One of the lead animals fell, kicking as it died. Walman also opened fire. Another animal went down. Yet the force of the stampede was too strong. They kept coming, trampling the downed animals without hesitation, bellowing, their horns gleaming sharp in the sunlight.

Devon ran, barely avoiding being knocked down. She heard the beast's harsh breathing, felt the brush of its massive shaggy body behind her. She stumbled on the rocks, scrambled desperately, and regained her footing, climbing faster than she thought possible, crowding Julia's heels. Danziger and Walman stopped shooting and ran for their lives as the main bulk of the herd came surging after the leaders.

Gaining a vantage point halfway up the ridge, Devon stopped and looked back, panting hard. The herd parted around the parked vehicles like water around a rock. Some of the beasts bellowed in fury and rammed the TransRover. The crash reverberated up the slopes. Devon was astonished to see the massive vehicle actually rock on its wheels.

Julia gripped her arm. "They're going to tip it over."

Devon's heart sank. "Oh, God, no," she whispered. She doubted even Danziger was ingenious enough to rig up a way to right the TransRover if it crashed over.

From the cab a small streak raced out and up the side to the top. True's voice, loud with anguish, carried over the deafening noise of the herd: "My koba!"

A crash and the rending screech of metal rocked the TransRover even harder. Some of the animals charged right over the top of the DuneRail. Others butted it, knocking it sideways. The TransRover continued to rock and sway, and the koba suddenly vanished from the top as though it had fallen off.

"No!" True cried.

She darted back down the hill, but Devon caught her. True swung her fists angrily, but Devon held on.

"Stop it!" she shouted at the girl. "You can't save the koba now. Listen to me! There's nothing you can do!"

True wrenched away, her face twisted with anguish, but she made no further attempt to move. Devon left her alone, knowing there was no comfort to offer right now.

She kept watching, unable to look away as their temporary camp was destroyed. Walman had run the opposite way and was crouched partway up the ridge on the other side of the herd. Danziger climbed toward Devon slowly. He still carried his rifle and was limping slightly.

Julia stepped forward to meet him, her eyes concerned. Some of her dark blond hair had fallen from its usual tidy bun. Her gorgeous face was streaked with dirt on one side and scratched on the other.

"You hurt?" she asked.

Danziger shook his head. His gaze went to True, who angrily avoided looking at him.

"I'd better check you anyway," Julia said, pulling out her med-scan.

"Just a sprain. Forget it," he growled and moved past her. "True, baby, I—"

"You could have let me get him," True said angrily. " I can run faster than you. I'd have made it."

"True—"

But the girl turned her back and scrambled up to the top of the ridge to join Uly and Yale. She stood there, not talking to anyone, her slim body stiff, the bill of her cap pulled low over her face.

Danziger glanced around, caught Devon's sympathetic gaze, and grimaced. "Damn," he said softly. He turned to watch the herd.

Most of it had passed now. Only a few stragglers brought up the rear; a dappled cow with a young calf, a crippled bull with streaks of white over its shoulders.

Danziger raised his rifle and shot down the latter. With a

moan, the old bull fell. "The meat'll probably be tough," Danziger said, "but we need food."

"Yeah," Devon said softly.

She started down the slope while the herd thundered on and the dust slowly settled. The primitive force of it, the suddenness of it, had left her feeling stunned, adrift.

She stopped beside the battered DuneRail and stared at its crumpled fender and torn seat without much comprehension.

The ground had been churned by hooves until it resembled a plowed field. Belongings were strewn in all directions, some of them trampled past recognition, others half-buried in the dirt, and others miraculously intact. The fans had been kicked around like balls. She bent and picked up one. Shaking it revealed a loud rattle inside like crushed glass. She frowned.

The others straggled down to join her. Their faces reflected shock. After a moment they began to sort slowly through the damage, searching for their possessions. Most things were still safely bundled in the cargo hold of the TransRover. But small items, some of them personal and therefore precious, had to be searched for.

Morgan sat down on one of the damaged fans and just stared. Bess began to search purposefully. Of them all, she looked the most calm. Then she bent and pulled something from the dirt. Holding it, she turned around.

"Morgan?" she called softly, then repeated with more urgency, "*Morgan?*"

Pressing her other hand to her face, she began to cry. He reached her before Devon could. Putting his arm around his wife, he held her tightly for a moment and gently took the broken item from her hand.

"What is it?" Devon asked.

Morgan held it out to show her. "A hologram of her family's home on Earth."

Bess wept harder against his shoulder. "I'll never see them again," she murmured through her tears. "I'll never see any of them again."

Devon's own eyes stung in sympathy. She found no words to say. However, the sunlight glinted on a corner of something sticking out of the ground. She bent and pulled it out. Brushing off the dust, she found another hologram box. It was intact. She shook it gently, and nothing rattled. Switching it on, she smiled at the image of a family group, and held it out.

"Bess," she said eagerly, "look."

Bess was still weeping and didn't respond.

Morgan shot Devon a grateful look and took the hologram by its base. "Bess, look," he said. "It's okay. You haven't lost them. Look."

Bess raised her tear-streaked face and stared in disbelief at first, then a smile broke through. She touched the little hologram, its light spinning across her fingers. "Oh," she breathed. "Oh."

Devon smiled and turned away, feeling her spirits starting to recover. No one was hurt. They could salvage this situation. They were going to be okay.

An angry chattering caught her attention just as True shrieked and went racing past.

"He's okay! My koba's okay!" she shouted. She dashed over to the gigantic wheel of the TransRover, and reached up for the small animal, which was scolding and hopping up and down on top of the wheel. "Come on," she crooned, a big grin splitting her face. "Come on down, you little monster, and I'll give you some fruit."

After a moment the little animal calmed down. It reached out its paw toward True, imitating her actions.

She scooped it into her arms and hugged it.

Uly bounced everywhere, climbing on top of the DuneRail like a young goat, then jumping off. "Wow!" he kept saying, his blue eyes huge in his face. The dust made him cough, but that barely slowed him down. "Wow! Mom, did you see how fast they could go? And those horns? Wow! They practically demolished this old thing." He kicked the fender of the DuneRail, making it clang loudly. "Maybe sometimes we could catch one, a baby one, and raise it. Maybe tame it and ride it. We could really zoom across this old desert then."

Devon glanced at the old cyborg tutor. "He's getting too excited. Maybe he'd better have some oxygen."

Yale nodded, but Uly scowled in protest. "I'm not a baby, Mom. I don't need it—" He broke off in another fit of coughing.

Devon caught Yale's eye. "Make sure Julia takes a look at him."

Yale nodded. His dark skin was coated with dust, and he still seemed a little out of breath himself. Pulling at the point of his goatee, he hesitated. "I will do so immediately," he said in his slow, formal way. "But first, I must have a word with you about the map."

She winced. "Yale, it's not your fault. Let's not go into that now."

"But the error could be mine," he said in concern. "I have given the matter considerable thought. It's possible I made a mistake."

"The probe was wrong about the mountains—"

"No. The probe is incapable of that kind of inaccuracy." Yale frowned. "However, as I recall, the data which registered was unclear. I decided the mass indicated was a mountain. Obviously I guessed erroneously." He looked ashamed. "I should have admitted this earlier."

Devon sighed, too tired to be angry. "At this point I don't think it makes much difference. The mountain's not the important issue anyway. It's the river we need to find."

Yale nodded and held out his hand to the boy. "Come, Uly. Let us do as your mother has said."

"Aw—"

"No arguments, please. Everyone has work to do. Obeying your mother is your task at the moment. Come."

He marched the boy off.

Devon turned around, trying to get organized in her mind. The first step was to assess the damage. As soon as possible they should move to a safer location.

Adjusting her gear to long range, she tried to call Alonzo. The pilot did not answer. Worriedly she checked his homing device. It was still active. So why didn't he answer?"

"Alonzo!" she said sharply. "We've had trouble here. Get back to camp right away—"

"Devon!"

It was Danziger's voice, urgent and sharper than usual.

Alarmed, Devon tossed down the battered canteen she was holding by its strap and raced to the TransRover. Danziger stood at the back of it, and when Devon reached him, she saw a puncture and long tear in one of the water tanks. A puddle spread beneath the vehicle. Even as she stared in dismay, the final ounces of water trickled into the puddle, then dripped, then ceased altogether.

Devon's mouth was suddenly paper dry. She swallowed with difficulty and forced herself to meet Danziger's grim eyes. "The other tank?"

"Intact," he replied.

She shut her eyes for a moment in sheer relief.

"It won't last long," he said. "We've got to find a source."

She nodded, his urgency and growing desperation mirrored in her. "I should have listened to you and stopped us on top of the ridge—"

"Don't second-guess yourself. It just wastes time, and we haven't any to spare," Danziger said.

"Devon, are you back here?" Coming around the corner, Julia stopped abruptly. She looked at their taut faces, then at the ground. Her eyes widened. "Oh, damn," she said.

Devon pushed past her own shock to take charge. "Run a quick check to see how many people still have their canteens. Everyone filled up before the charge, didn't they?"

Julia nodded slowly, still staring at the mud. "I think so."

"Then that's all they get for the rest of the day. One canteen a day," Devon said grimly.

Julia's eyes met hers. "But we'll be to the river soon—"

Devon shook her head. "We have a bigger problem, but I don't want to address that with everyone until we've gathered up our belongings and are up on that ridge. Check the water please."

Julia pulled herself together and nodded. "Yes, at once. Your son—"

"Yes?" Devon asked anxiously.

"He's fine. No need for oxygen. I just wanted to reassure you."

Devon relaxed only a fraction. She nodded, relieved about Uly, but too worried about the water to smile. "Thank you."

Julia shot her another look, clearly wanting to ask questions, but aware that action was needed now more than talk. "I'll get to work," she said and hurried off.

But in minutes everyone knew about the ruptured water tank. Not everyone had had his or her canteen clipped on when the herd came through. Some of the canteens had been trampled too severely for salvage; others were battered but okay. Morgan sloshed his and clipped it on, his eyes following Devon as she rounded everyone up and issued orders.

Slowly the scattered remnants of their belongings were gathered, at least those items still usable. Zero popped out the crushed fender on the DuneRail. One of the solar panels was cracked, but the vehicle was still functional. Devon climbed onto the seat with a subdued Bess beside her, gunned the DuneRail up the slope to the top of the ridge, and idled there until the TransRover lumbered up beside her.

From this vantage point the plains looked empty, but they knew better now. To the southwest a dark cloud moved slowly along the horizon. Devon frowned at it, recognizing it as the dust Alonzo had been so curious about. She tried calling him again, but got no answer.

Frustrated and worried about him, she tried not to imagine the pilot caught and trampled by another herd of the buffalo creatures.

Meanwhile, everyone gathered around the DuneRail. In silence they stared at Devon, waiting for the bad news.

She told them, playing it straight, showing them the map, telling them the problem as matter-of-factly as possible. They listened without interruption, but the shock in their faces said enough.

Scowling, Morgan kicked the ground. "Then this is all Yale's fault. If he hadn't—"

"No," Devon said with a quick glance at the tutor. "We just need to search for a different geological feature, that's all. As for the damage we've sustained—"

"Those stupid animals," Morgan said. "If they hadn't ruptured the water tank, we'd be all right."

"No, Morgan. We have no way of knowing now when we'll find water. The buffaloes just speeded up the deadline. They didn't cause the problem."

"How long can we go without water, in this heat?" Bess asked.

Devon glanced at Julia, who said, "Humans can survive without food more easily than they can do without water. The heat is a factor we can't ignore. We're going to have to conserve our energy more than before. Get out of this blazing sunlight, for starters. Travel only by night."

"But that will take longer," True said, ignoring her father's frown. The koba sat on her shoulder, watching them with bright, beady eyes. "We need to travel quicker, don't we? To find water sooner?"

"At this point, survival and conservation are more important," Julia replied. "If Alonzo has scouted a day's journey for us already without finding anything, then we shouldn't gamble on—"

"Where is Solace anyway?" Morgan demanded. "I thought he was just making a little circle to check the malfunction on the ATV. Why isn't he back by now? He should be here, helping."

"I'm glad he was gone when the buffaloes hit," Danziger said gruffly. "One less damaged vehicle to repair."

"Maybe," Morgan grumbled. "Or maybe he—"

"He's coming!" Uly sang out. The boy pointed excitedly. "Look!"

Everyone turned toward the west. Devon saw a streak of red coming at maximum speed, dust boiling behind it. She let out a sigh of relief and saw Julia relax visibly. At least he was all right.

"Decision," Danziger said, bringing Devon's mind back to the problem at hand. "Do we go on, or do we wait until dark? If we wait, I need to open the cocoon unit and give us some shade."

Devon's gaze sought Julia's. The doctor shrugged. "I've already said what my—"

"What about the dark?" Morgan broke in. "What if those things run at night? We can't see them. We could—"

"I think we're safe as long as we stay on high ground," Devon said.

Morgan glared at her. "And you're an expert on this life form and its habits? You know for certain they always run along canyons and valleys, never going over a ridge? I don't think 'safe' is a word that applies to anything in this situation."

"But that could be the only herd," Bess said softly.

Devon's gaze moved to the dust cloud on the far horizon, but she said nothing.

"We've survived so far, with no one hurt," Bess went on. "God is looking after us. We have to be able to trust in that assurance."

"Right now we need more than faith," Morgan said. "We need concrete facts."

"Devon?" Danziger said.

They all looked at her. She drew a deep breath. "Set up the tent," she said. "As soon as it's dark, we'll move onward."

Danziger nodded and headed off, still limping but not letting it slow him down. "True," he said, "you can help me."

She followed more slowly, the koba still perched on her shoulder. Danziger glanced back and paused until she caught up. He patter her other shoulder briefly and said something to her that made her look up at him.

Devon climbed down off the DuneRail and stretched wearily. Her brain felt dulled by the heat. It was hard to think.

"Yale!" she said.

The old Teacher gave Uly a pat on the shoulder and came over to her, eyes down as though he expected a reprimand. In his youth Yale had committed a political crime and had been blanked and reconditioned into a Teacher. Although he had lost all knowledge of who he had been or what crime he had committed, in return his brain contained implants of entire encyclopedias of knowledge. In Devon's childhood, when he'd been her tutor, he'd seemed to know everything. Now she looked fondly at the old cyborg, well aware of how outdated he was, as robotic teachers went. Yet she wouldn't trade him in for the world, and neither would Uly.

"We've got to institute strict water rationing," she told him. "Just issuing a canteen each day isn't accurate enough. I'd like for you to compute how many liters we've got left and redetermine our rationing allotments."

"Of course," Yale said without hesitation. He brightened slightly, realizing that she still trusted his capabilities. "For how many days?"

She swallowed, feeling that if she chose a deadline, it might well be their last day. Frowning, she shook off her fears. "Ten days tops," she said, knowing it was too long. "Then work back from that maximum. I want a chart of all possibilities within that framework. We'll have another meeting later and vote on what we want to do."

"Very well," Yale said. "A suitable mathematical problem for Uly to work on."

"No way!" Uly said immediately. "I've got to go help True."

"Mathematics is the fulcrum to understanding the entire universe," Yale said and led the protesting boy away.

Devon watched them, but Julia approached her, and she turned wearily to confront the next set of problems. "Thank goodness no one got hurt . . . or killed," Devon said. "How about John's ankle?"

The doctor wiped her face, leaving sweaty streaks of dirt

and grime across it. "I haven't had a chance to check it. He's too busy." She rolled her eyes with mock exasperation, and for a moment Devon could almost smile.

Julia's own gaze remained west, where Alonzo was still streaking toward them. "We were lucky," she said. "Medical supplies are limited despite what we recovered from those Grendlers a few weeks ago. Living without any cytokine tabs at all makes me nervous. I don't want anyone to have to suffer the way Alonzo did while his legs healed naturally."

"I guess being at the top of your class didn't exactly prepare you for old-fashioned frontier medicine," Devon said.

Julia flushed, instantly defensive. "I know my job," she said. "Surely I've proven that by now."

Devon nodded. "You have. Sorry."

For a moment there was only tense silence between them, then Julia sighed. "Escaping this heat is imperative. That one water tank is less than half-full. Evaporation will be a factor. And we need more than drinking water. There's cooking to be done, and washing."

"We don't need to be clean," Devon said harshly. "We need to survive."

Both women stared at the dust cloud on the horizon, the thunder of hooves still echoing through their minds. They could have all been caught and trampled to death, Devon thought grimly.

"There's something else I wanted to say," Julia said hesitantly.

Devon glanced at her, brows lifted.

Julia met her eyes briefly then looked down. "Sending Uly to me for oxygen—"

"You said he was okay." Devon was instantly concerned. "Does he need to go back on his breathing apparatus?"

"No. He—"

"I thought his lungs needed checking. With all this dust, he's been coughing a lot. There's been far too much excitement and he's getting tired. I don't want to risk—"

"Devon, that's my point. Uly's fine."

"He was coughing."

"So's everyone else. That's normal."

Devon shook her head.

Julia frowned at her. "He's no more tired than anyone else. You're overreacting again. He didn't need checking at all."

"That happens to be your primary job, Doctor," Devon said angrily. "It's why you were hired, remember? To take care of Uly until he can be back with Dr. Vasquez."

"I have a medical responsibility for everyone in this group," Julia said with equal heat. "Not just your son."

Devon's face flamed. "I didn't mean you should neglect the others."

"Your son happens to be fine. Stop babying him!" Julia said in exasperation. "The boy is getting stronger every day, but he can't make the progress we want if you continue to hold him back."

"I'm not holding him back," Devon retorted. "I'm looking out for his welfare, and that's your responsibility too. Or have you forgotten?"

"I haven't forgotten that you don't trust my judgment or my ability to treat him to your specifications," Julia said icily. "I don't appreciate having to continually justify my qualifications."

"Then take care of him," Devon said, and spun away.

"I *will*," Julia said to her back. "When he needs it. Right now he doesn't."

Devon shut her eyes for a moment and tried to calm

down. "Okay," she said without turning around. "I'm overreacting."

"It's understandable," Julia said. "But for Uly's sake, you have to loosen the strings. He needs confidence in himself and his own health. He can achieve that if you set him an example."

"Okay," Devon whispered. "Noted. I'll try."

Julia started to say something else, but Alonzo roared up in a cloud of dust.

"Where have you been?" Devon demanded. "Is something wrong with your gear? Weren't you getting my transmissions?"

He shook his head. He was completely coated with dust, to the point of being unrecognizable, except for his fiery dark eyes. They flashed at her with mischief now, and he drove a tall staff into the ground at her feet. A colored scrap of leather fluttered from the other end, and some beads made from polished bone clacked softly against the wood.

"What is this?" Devon asked in astonishment. She pulled up the staff and hefted it in her hand. It was taller than she. "Terrian?"

Alonzo nodded. He held up another object. This was a long femur bone, also presumably Terrian, but blackened as though it had been in a fire. One end had been carved with deep, slashing cuts. The other end was caked with dried dirt as though it had been stuck in the ground for a long time.

"Those are Grendler markings," Julia said.

Alonzo nodded again. Without a word he held up a third item. It was a skull, long and narrow and Terrian. Like the femur, it was also burned black.

Julia took it from him and turned it over in her hands. "This has been outside a long time," she said. "It takes years to weather bone to this degree. In this harsh light it should be bleached though."

Grendler markings had been carved on the top of it.

"Where did you find these things?" Devon asked.

Alonzo pointed west over his shoulder. "About seven klicks from here there's a road of sorts."

"A road!" Devon exclaimed.

"Not paved or anything. Not used recently either, but a definite track. It heads toward where our mountains should be. I didn't find them."

"No," Devon said softly. "We found out there are no mountains."

"Figures," he said without curiosity. "Anyway, this stuff was just out there in the middle of the road." Alonzo frowned and turned the femur over in his hands. "I can't explain it, but I just have the feeling these objects are a warning. A sort of primitive beacon that means 'stay away.' Then just a short ways on, the ground drops off to a wide, shallow valley with some cliffs on the other side."

"Is there a river?" Devon and Julia said simultaneously.

Alonzo shook his head. "Not even a channel or a dry bed. Just these big dust wallows and a lot of trampled weeds."

"We know about trampled," Julia muttered.

"But the sensors indicated water," he went on.

Devon perked up, and Julia's hand gripped the back of Alonzo's seat.

"Water?" Devon echoed. "Where?"

He swept his hands back through his hair and shrugged. "Hard to pinpoint it. The nav units aren't the only thing on this baby showing wear."

Devon felt impatience choking her. She tried to hold it down. "So what are you saying? Did you locate water or not?"

His dark eyes met hers. "The sensors indicate water on the other side of the valley, but I couldn't pinpoint a precise

40

location. The information kept breaking up, almost as though a magnetic field of some kind was interfering."

Devon nodded to herself. "That was John's theory." She squinted out across the plains, straining to see to the far, far distance through the water mirages shimmering in the heat.

"Or maybe it's underground. I don't know. Sorry," Alonzo said.

Devon grinned. "I'm not sorry. I'm glad. Good work. Now we have something definite to shoot for."

Alonzo glanced around. "Looks like you ran into trouble while I was gone."

Devon's relief had her grinning. Right then the damages they'd sustained seemed like nothing. "We were nearly run down by a herd of—"

"I saw them," he said. "Big and shaggy and ugly."

She nodded.

He glanced at Julia. "Anyone hurt?"

"No. But the TransRover—"

He turned to look at the huge machine.

"It sustained serious damage to the water tanks," Devon said. "We lost half our water supply."

He stared at her in consternation. "Oh, hell."

"We're on tight rationing. Danziger is putting up the tent for shade. We plan to wait until dark, then move on. And now that we know for certain there's—"

"You can't," Alonzo said.

Devon's eagerness slowly faded. Puzzled, she stared at him. "Explain. You said you'd found water."

"Yeah, I said maybe. But that's not the problem." He twisted in the seat and pointed at the dust. "See that cloud?"

"I was hoping it meant rain," Julia said.

Alonzo snorted. "Sorry, *querida*. The herd you encountered, was it going that way?"

41

Devon pointed. "It followed the curve of this little canyon."

"Then it was going to the others."

"What others?" Julia asked.

Devon broke in before he could reply. "You mean there's another herd?"

His eyes were serious for once. "Bigger than a herd. Bigger than you can imagine. Infinite numbers of them, like the stars. I got cut off for a while, between these little feeder herds that are going to it, or I'd have been back sooner. We have to find another direction. The west is cut off, at least for now."

Stubbornness settled over Devon like a net. "We can't. We have no alternative but to proceed. You know that."

"Can't we go around them?" Julia asked.

Alonzo shrugged.

Devon was thinking hard. "Has the main herd already cut us off?"

"It's there." He pointed southward at the dust. "The road across the valley is over there." He swung around and pointed farther northwest. "I'm not saying we have to take the road, but it would be easier for the TransRover to get up and down those steep slopes."

Devon measured the difference with her eyes, calculating rapidly. "Then possibly we might get across before they cut us off," she said.

"Maybe. It's a big risk. Better to wait."

Bitterness welled up in Devon. "For how long?"

He shrugged again. "Hard to say. A few hours, maybe a day."

"We can wait a day," Julia said. "We have enough water for that."

"And after a day?" Devon asked worriedly. "What if we

42

decide to wait, and they keep coming? What if we can't get across?"

"Oh, we'll get across," Julia said confidently. "I know this herd seemed to go past us forever, but it was really only about ten or fifteen minutes. Adrenaline affects your sense of time—"

"I know that," Devon said impatiently. She looked at Alonzo.

He said, "I can't estimate the size, but I think it will take them a very long time to cross. I never saw so many animals."

"Yale calls them buffalo," Julia said.

Alonzo frowned, turning the word over as though he'd never heard it before. "Strange name."

"Strange animals," Devon said dryly. "We don't have days to wait. It must be a massive migration, probably something seasonal. Meanwhile, we could be stranded here while our water runs out. We can't risk that."

"But you're risking putting us in even greater danger," Julia said.

"I can run some calculations on the nav unit," Alonzo offered. "Do a projection of our chances of getting across based on the buffaloes' current rate of speed versus what we can do."

"Okay," Devon said, grateful for his support. "That would be useful. Julia, tell the others what's going on."

Julia adjusted her gear and started talking.

Alonzo went to work. Devon leaned over the dash of the ATV watching the data entries flash across the dusty screen. After a moment Alonzo paused, frowning at the readout.

He looked up. "If we do it, we have to hurry. At best, it'll be very close."

Danziger and Morgan came over to join them in time to

hear what Alonzo had said. Danziger was frowning, and Morgan looked alarmed.

"Devon, are you seriously considering this madness?" Morgan demanded.

She nodded, and Danziger said, "We don't have a lot of choice."

"Of course we have a choice," Morgan said. "We can wait until the buffaloes go by. That's Julia's suggestion, and I think it's sound."

"And if it's a major migration?" Devon asked. "How long do we wait?"

"Every moment we debate is another moment lost," Danziger said.

Morgan turned on him. "You aren't seriously considering going along with this, are you?"

Danziger shook his head. "Not considering, no."

Morgan relaxed. "Good. Because it's crazy—"

"I've already made up my mind. Devon's right," Danziger said. "We have to try."

Morgan's jaw dropped open. "No!"

Danziger's gaze swept around and locked on Devon's. "We've got a slow leak in the seam line of the other water tank," he said. "I've applied a cold patch, but it won't hold more than a few hours."

Devon's eyes widened with dismay. *What else?* she wondered, then hastily pulled herself together.

"I say we should vote," Morgan said angrily. "Everyone is tired and hot and still shaken. We're not up to another crisis."

"There's no need for a vote," Devon said. "We've no choice now."

Danziger nodded and hastened away.

Morgan glared after him. "Come back here! We haven't finished—"

"It's already decided," Alonzo said softly.

"Danziger!" Morgan shouted. "I'm not finished with you!"

Danziger kept walking and never looked back.

Morgan slammed his fist down on a bar of the ATV. "Devon, this is insanity. We can't—"

"Talking wastes time," Alonzo said softly to Devon.

She nodded. "Morgan, I'm sorry, but we can't survive if we don't have water."

Julia said, "I'll help the others get ready."

Alonzo went with her, leaving Devon and Morgan glaring at each other.

"I tell you it's a stupid risk," Morgan said. "I won't take it, and neither will my wife. We all need rest, a chance to—"

"Morgan, this isn't like the station," Devon said wearily. "By now you should understand you can't just turn a tap and have water come out the end. We have to provide for ourselves, protect ourselves."

"Exactly. But you want to take us on a wild goose chase that will only bring us face-to-face with those animals. We were lucky once. How do you know we'll be that lucky again?"

"Okay," Devon said. "Maybe we'll get caught halfway across the valley and maybe we'll be trampled to death. Maybe we won't. But if the patch on the tank fails, the water that's in your canteen right now, *right now*," she repeated, "will be all you'll have to drink until you die, sitting right here waiting for a safer opportunity to come along."

Shock flared in his eyes. He stared at her, blinking, then he attempted to rally. "But you have no guarantee of water past the valley. You can't know for sure—"

Devon stamped her foot on the hard ground. "This ground is certain," she said. "Right here, at this spot, we have little shelter, practically no water, and only the prospect of things getting worse. Out there—" she pointed west—"is hope. I'd rather risk everything on hope than die of certainty. Wouldn't you?"

Morgan frowned. He didn't look convinced. "But . . ."

Devon tossed the Terrian and Grendler items on the DuneRail's seat and climbed in. "We've come too far to give up. Let's not die here, Morgan, hopeless and helpless. Let's at least give it a shot."

"This is foolish," Morgan said sharply. "You can talk the others into it, but you haven't convinced me. It's a mad chase in the noonday heat, and for what? *What*, Devon?"

Devon turned her head to meet Morgan's angry eyes. "Life," she said simply and started the DuneRail's engine.

Chapter 3

• • • • • • ● ●

The race began, a slow, strange race whose progress could be marked only by the scanner screens as they tracked the main buffalo herd. As many people as possible crammed the seats of the DuneRail and cab of the TransRover. The rest alternately jogged and walked. Julia, clocking them anxiously, called out rest periods and passed out salt tablets.

The big, slow TransRover hampered them the most. Devon gripped the wheel of the ATV too tightly, feeling urgency beating inside her. Now and then she forced her grip to loosen, forced herself to take it easy. Everyone was doing his or her best. If they didn't make it, they didn't make it.

But with every klick passed, Morgan's words echoed louder in Devon's ears.

What if they didn't make it? What if the speed they were

maintaining over rough terrain cracked the patch of the tank? What if Alonzo's readings of water were wrong? What if Alonzo's calculations were wrong, and they didn't make it?

One problem at a time, she told herself, pushing the doubts and worries away. Right now, her job was to follow Alonzo as he led them west.

"Rest!" Julia called over the gear. "Break, everyone. Now."

Reluctantly Devon braked the ATV and turned the wheel over to Bess, who was sitting next to her. Devon scrambled out and accepted a salt tablet from Julia, putting the bitter wafer under her tongue. She was tempted to take a sip from her canteen, but she resisted it. Instead, she licked some of the sweat from her lips and fanned herself with her hat.

On her gear she called ahead to Alonzo. "How're we doing?"

"Two klicks from the edge," he reported back.

She could see the yellow DuneRail perched halfway up a low slope, its solar panels gilded by the sunlight. Her skin felt parched, like leather. Ahead of her a mirage shimmered. She licked her lips again and looked for the dust cloud. It seemed no closer than before, and although she knew she couldn't reliably judge distances with her naked eye in this featureless terrain, she took hope. Maybe they were going to make it.

"Okay, everyone set?" she asked over her gear. "Let's go."

It was her turn to run instead of ride. Within a few paces, her heart hammered in her chest like a gong and her legs burned with exhaustion. She could hear herself puffing loudly beneath the cloth tied over her nose and mouth, just like everyone else.

Behind her, the TransRover loomed against the sky, its engine noise deafening as it strained to keep up.

Overhead, a bird wheeled in black silhouette. Insects buzzed and jumped ahead of the vehicles. But they saw no other signs of life, not even the funny little burrowing creatures that had seemed so plentiful yesterday. Now and then Devon caught the sound of a low rumble, and her heart jerked in panicky anticipation of another stampede.

"Look!" Baines called.

Their heads turned in the direction he was pointing. Devon saw a herd of buffalo streaming over a distant ridge, heading toward the cloud. This far away, she could see the animals' strange gracefulness which belied their big, awkward bodies and spindly legs. They ran like a stream of gray liquid, and she could hear the faint thunder of their passing.

The sun dipped lower, hot and bright in their faces as they swung due west behind Alonzo. A breeze started up, blowing hot and dry, giving little relief. Behind the Trans-Rover the wind circled and caught up a column of dust in a momentary spout that died again quickly.

Devon's nostrils were filled with the bitter scent of crushed weeds.

"Heads up, everyone!" Alonzo's voice came over her gear. "We're on the road."

It was heartening encouragement. Devon felt a new surge of energy, and she watched carefully until she saw the weeds abruptly part. The road was simply sun-baked mud, much cracked and worn, but no vegetation grew across it, and they all quickened their pace as the vehicles lumbered onto the surface.

Ahead of her the ATV suddenly braked to a halt. Bess scrambled out, clutching the staff and bones that Alonzo had collected. She put them back on the ground, pushing the bone into the hard earth as far as she could, then supporting it at its base with the skull.

"Don't fool with that nonsense," Morgan snapped, but Bess ignored him.

"Whatever it is, it's important," she insisted. "It's been here a long time, and if it's a warning, then the next travelers after us need to see it."

Morgan snorted and shook his head, but Bess got back in the ATV and rolled on.

Following in her dust, Devon shuffled past the totems with a frown of uneasiness. They were very strange, all right. She was glad Bess had replaced them.

"Making good time," Alonzo said, his voice encouraging them all.

Then, just when Devon's legs threatened to give under her and little black spots were dancing in front of her vision, they reached the edge of the valley.

In wonder, they all stopped near where the road dipped down the slope, and gazed out across the ancient cut in the earth that nature had carved long ago. It was like a mighty canyon that had been widened and widened over the passage of time. At least a klick wide and fairly shallow, it was bordered on the far side by stone cliffs and overhangs.

Devon stared, feeling the rapid beat of her heart, and for a moment her imagination seemed to hear ancient drums. There was something incredibly old about this valley, something indefinable she couldn't describe, yet she felt it strongly. A response stirred in her blood, and she found herself shivering uneasily.

Uly crowded against her, and she put her hands on his shoulders as he stood in front of her, his boots planted firmly on the hard-packed earth. She bent over him, and he flashed her a quick grin. His blue eyes shone eagerly as he drank in the sight of the valley.

"I wish it was green," he whispered. "Green from things growing everywhere. And vines hanging off the cliffs, kind of like in a jungle only not as thick. And flowers on the vines, white and purple, maybe, or brighter so the bees and insects will come to them. Blue and green birds everywhere, singing, and the river flowing at the bottom . . ."

His voice trailed off, and for an instant Devon could almost see the valley as he envisioned it: alive, peaceful, lovely.

Then she shivered, and all she saw was dying weeds, dust, and the stones. Devon blinked and wiped her face, feeling slightly disoriented.

She swept her gaze left, anxiously searching for sight of the coming buffalo. She couldn't see them, but she could hear the rumbling sound of their hooves. It awakened dread inside her. The cloud filled the sky to the south, dark with dust, as though a storm were coming.

Her hands tightened on Uly's thin shoulders. "We have to hurry," she said aloud.

As though everyone else had also been under a spell, they stirred and looked around. Alonzo drove the DuneRail forward to the edge and started to go down.

"Wait!" Julia shouted.

Devon looked around and saw her pointing at a lone, squat figure hurrying toward them from the north.

"Where did it come from?" Uly asked.

Devon swallowed her impatience. "I don't know, but we aren't hanging around if it wants to chat. Alonzo, go on—"

The Grendler waved and shouted something they were too far away to hear.

Alonzo hesitated, glancing over his shoulder. Behind them, Danziger was climbing down from the cab of the TransRover.

"Morgan," Devon said with a sigh, "better see what it wants. But be quick about it."

She glanced south and could see a gray shadow in the distance, a shadow that was spreading across the ground. She blinked, her mouth falling open in astonishment. *Infinite,* Alonzo had said, and he hadn't exaggerated much.

"They're coming," Devon said.

The others looked, and Devon heard gasps.

"We're too late," Bess said.

"Too late," Julia agreed.

The men exchanged quick glances, and Alonzo's hand dropped off the controls of the DuneRail.

"Hey!" the Grendler called, still hurrying their way. It waved again. "Hey!"

Morgan turned and almost tripped over his own feet as he stared at the oncoming buffalo. Then he regained his balance and hurried toward the Grendler, his ponytail bobbing behind him.

He held up his hand. "Hey!" he called back. It was the closest any of them could approximate the standard Grendler greeting.

At his approach, the Grendler abruptly stopped in its tracks and squatted in the dust. Its long-fingered hand swept across the dust, back and forth, indicating that it wanted to talk and possibly trade. Devon watched a moment, then found herself irresistibly drawn back to staring at the buffaloes.

The animals filled the entire breadth of the valley, crammed shoulder to shoulder, so close it seemed their horns would lock together. Teaming, they came, a solid gray mass of muscle and primitive force.

Already, although they were not yet close, Devon could feel a tremor in the ground. She stepped away from the edge of the slope.

"We'd better back away," she said. "Don't want to risk tangling with any strays."

But Danziger stood at her shoulder, still watching the animals come. His craggy face was set grimly. "We could try to cross," he said. "The distance is deceiving. Just because you can see them now doesn't mean they're all that close."

"But they're moving fast," she countered. "What if we get halfway across and they catch up with us? We wouldn't have a chance."

"Devon!" Morgan shouted.

She turned around and saw him gesturing urgently at her. Quickly she strode over to where he crouched before the Grendler. She squatted too, her nostrils wrinkling at the creature's unwashed stench. The Grendler was grunting in agitation and gesturing quickly. With its staff it pointed at the valley and shook its other hand.

"No go," it grunted. "No go."

"Yeah, no kidding," Morgan muttered. "Like we'd be stupid enough to go down in there now with those things coming."

He rolled his eyes Devon's way, and she sighed. "Right," she said. "We're not that stupid."

Relief flashed in Morgan's face before he turned back to the Grendler. "No go," he agreed.

The Grendler leaned back on its haunches and rapped the end of its staff on the ground as though in satisfaction. "Huh," it grunted. "Huh."

"What's it want?" Devon asked.

Morgan frowned. "We haven't gotten that far yet. You in a hurry, or something?"

She glanced over her shoulder, feeling resignation seep through her tired muscles. She was so thirsty her tongue felt like sandpaper. Water was all she could think about. Defeat was something she'd never been comfortable with. "Damn," she said softly.

"I thought you'd want to ask it about the nearest place to get water," Morgan said.

Devon's attention refocused. She nodded at him. "Yes. Good."

But the Grendler stared at them without comprehension. Morgan pantomimed everything he could think of, and still the Grendler didn't respond.

The Grendler stared at Devon with avid eyes. "Deal," it said.

"Yes," she said quickly. "We'll make a deal if you'll take us to water." As she spoke, she pointed across the valley.

The Grendler waved its staff. "No go. No *go!*"

She eyed it with frustration. "Then where can we find water?"

It made no answer, and she unclipped her canteen. Squirting out a few precious drops of the tepid liquid, she extended her hand. "Water."

"Ah." The Grendler pursed its lips and touched a clawed fingertip to her wet palm. Almost reverently it traced a glistening line across its knobby brow, then stared up at the sky. It said something incomprehensible and extended its palm upward.

"We're getting nowhere," Morgan muttered restlessly. "Maybe this one's got a case of sunstroke."

But the Grendler lowered its gaze. "Deal," it said.

"If you show us water," Devon said, "what do you want in exchange?"

"Bottom line," Morgan said. "What do you want to deal?"

The Grendler loosed a raspy chuckle. "Bottom line," it said. It poked Morgan in the chest with its staff, knocking him back. "Heard of bottom line. No good deal made with bottom line."

"Then deal with me," Devon said before Morgan could respond. "If you take us to water, what do you want for it?"

The Grendler's gaze moved avidly to her waist. Her hand closed over her Mag-Pro. "No weapons," she said involuntarily. "We need those."

"Need water," the Grendler said.

"Not that much," she countered. "We know there's water across the valley." As she spoke, she pointed.

Again the Grendler seemed alarmed. It shook its staff in warning. "No go!" it shouted.

"What is it, sacred or something?" Morgan said in exasperation. He glanced at Devon from the corner of his eye. "Of course we have some leverage here. We don't have to make a deal at all with this character if we don't want to."

She nodded.

They stared at the Grendler, who glared back.

"Mag-Pro," it muttered.

Devon shook her head. "No."

"Here," Morgan said, pulling an object from his pocket. It was the broken hologram of Bess's home on Earth. He held it up, turning it so the sun's reflection flashed along the small rectangle's length. He also held it so the Grendler couldn't see its broken side. "Pretty, isn't it?"

The Grendler stared at it, seemingly interested, then pointed at Devon's gun again. "Mag-Pro," it said.

Devon stood up in disgust. "This guy has a one-track mind. No—"

"Wait." Morgan put away the broken hologram and pulled out the one that still worked. He switched it on, and the small figures of Bess's family came to life suddenly.

The Grendler emitted a startled whistle and jumped back. Morgan chuckled. "Scared you, didn't it?" He held it up and turned it around so the Grendler could see all sides of the shimmering figures. Then he put his hand through it. "Pretty good magic, isn't it?"

The Grendler crept closer again. Its gaze was riveted to the hologram.

"You like this, don't you?" Morgan said, his voice coaxing. "You take us to water, and you can have a hologram."

"Hologram," the Grendler echoed.

"That's right. Good deal. Water for hologram."

The Grendler scowled and pulled out an object from its tattered clothing. It laid it on the ground, then watched them eagerly.

Devon recognized the battered object as a medical probe. Anger shot through her. "More of our missing med supplies," she said. "Damn them—"

"Never mind," Morgan said. His gaze remained on the Grendler as he shook his head. "No deal. We don't need that. Water for hologram."

The Grendler pushed the probe across the dusty ground toward him and reached out eagerly for the hologram.

Morgan held it out of reach, and the Grendler grunted angrily.

"No deal," Morgan repeated. "We want water, not this." As he spoke, he pushed the probe back toward the Grendler.

"Bottom line always want ship things," the Grendler said hoarsely. "Bottom line always trade."

"Not this time," Morgan said. "We don't want to cross the valley unless we have to. We need water, and there's water over there."

"No go—"

"We *will* go," Devon said harshly, "just as soon as the buffalo are gone. We will go, to find water. No deal."

The Grendler scowled. "You trade this thing. You trade!"

It picked up the probe and gestured. "Probe for hologram. Water for Mag-Pro."

Devon forgot to breathe for a second. She and Morgan exchanged glances.

Morgan frowned at her. "Just remove the ammo and hand it over," he urged softly.

"No," she said, wondering if she were signing their death warrants. "We're committed to not giving them weapons. Gaal does enough of that already."

"To hell with policy," Morgan said urgently. "You were making speeches about survival, remember? You were ready to risk our lives out there with those buffalo, and now you stick because of some stupid principle?"

She bit her lip, feeling the force of his argument. Hesitating, she turned back to the Grendler. "Water, how far?" she asked.

The Grendler didn't respond. Morgan made the sign language for "days," and the Grendler counted them off.

"Good deal," it said. "Much water. Mag-Pro needed. Good deal, all side."

"No," Devon said, disappointment making her voice harsh.

"But, Devon—"

"I said no! It's too far. Too many days. We have a better chance right here."

Morgan looked as though he wanted to argue with her, but he didn't. Compressing his lips, he swung back to the Grendler and made the sign for "no." "No deal," he said.

"Hah!" Angrily the Grendler slammed its staff on the ground, nearly rapping it across Morgan's feet, then it scrambled up and waddled away on its broad, three-toed feet. In a few moments, it whirled around and glared at them. "No go!" it shouted, pointing with its staff at the valley. "All die, go there. No go!"

It shouted something else, but by then the rumble was loud and growing louder. As the Grendler scuttled away, the vanguard of the herd came hurtling up the valley, and the Grendler's final words of warning to them were drowned out in the thunder of the animals' passing.

Although the group was safely out of range and in no danger, they involuntarily backed away from the edge. The dust cloud came with the animals, and suddenly a fog seemed to descend over all of them. Visibility fell to a few feet. Coughing and squinting, they stumbled into one another as they struggled to erect the big geodesic tent for shelter. Even with it sealed, the dust came seeping in. The interior of the tent held a faint haziness that grew thicker. The men put on environmental masks and took turns keeping watch outside in case any buffalo tried to run through the camp. Bess and Julia worked on preparing something to eat. No one seemed very hungry, especially when there was nothing to drink with the meal.

Devon paced the perimeter of the tent, weary but unable to rest. The constant, deafening noise outside kept her restless and on edge. She made sure Uly was bedded down for a nap with Yale to guard him. True and her koba tagged along at Devon's heels.

"Do you think they're going to come up here and get us?" True asked.

"No," Devon reassured her. "We're okay."

"But there's a lot of them. Maybe they won't stay in the valley. Maybe it's not big enough for all of them."

It was unlike True to show worry. Devon glanced down at the girl and saw her eyes wide and luminous over the cloth tied across the bottom half of her face. The koba seemed fascinated by her mask. It kept patting the cloth, then putting its paws across its own muzzle.

Angry bellows in the distance made True flinch. "They sound kind of mad."

"I guess they are, but all we have to worry about up here is not choking on the dust and not going deaf listening to them."

Julia set up the lamps, and True watched her. "It's almost like it's getting dark outside. But it's not night yet."

"No, not yet." Devon patted her shoulder. "Why don't you tell me how the patch on the tank is holding?"

At once True brightened. "Okay. Dad did a good job with it. I helped. It works pretty good 'cause it's pliable, but it gets harder the longer it's on. It's just for temporary holding, see? And that's why it won't last very long."

"Can your father put on another one?"

"Maybe." True shrugged. "He said the material doesn't bond very well with itself, but he's going to try." She put the koba on her shoulder, stroked it, and frowned to herself.

"He's pretty clever about finding a way to get the job done," Devon said, reassuring herself as much as the child.

"Yeah." True glanced away, looking troubled by something.

Devon didn't press her. There were too many things to worry about just then.

"Want to go outside and look at it?" True asked. "I can show you where we—"

The flap to the tent zipped open and Walman staggered in. A mound of dirt spilled in with him, falling off his shoulders, puffing from his boot tops, coating his clothing. He coughed and pulled off his environmental mask, scrubbing his face with the back of his hand, and then staggered over to get some food.

Devon put her hand on True's shoulder. "No," she said quietly. "I don't think going outside is a very good idea right now."

As she spoke, she glanced up at the pale material of the tent. It seemed like a flimsy shelter from what raged outside.

Walman took a swallow of water, rinsed his mouth with it, and spat. They all stared at him, and he grimaced as he realized what he'd done.

"Sorry," he said to Devon. "I, uh, got a message from Solace. He checked the scanners, and he says the animals are still coming. Probably for hours, is his estimation."

Her heart sank. Hours of deafening noise, hours of enduring the tremor in the ground that felt like an earthquake, hours of choking dust, hours while their water diminished ounce by ounce.

But she tried to keep her reaction contained inside. She gave Walman a nod of thanks and smiled at True.

"It's going to go on all night, isn't it?" True asked worriedly. "It might go on forever."

"Not forever," Devon said, aware that the others were listening, drawing reassurance from her, wanting to believe her. "But I guess we're going to have a long, noisy night."

Chapter 4

• • • • • • • ● ●

Holding his Mag-Pro in one hand and his torch in the other, Alonzo paced slowly along the western side of the tent. The all-encompassing dust made the darkness even thicker, and the two moons overhead glowed dimly, all but obscured from sight.

He paused at the end of his sentry line to turn back, then leaned his shoulder against the tent's corner frame and gazed up at the sky. Tonight, with the herd bellowing and rumbling down in the valley, the tremors in the ground constant beneath his boot soles, the rasp of his mask respirator steady in his ears, he had never felt so trapped or so far away from the space he loved more than anything else.

Usually during the day he could keep himself too busy to think about it, but nights were the worst. At night he could see the stars, set like jewels in the black velvet of infinity. The constellations here had grown familiar to him. While the others slept, he would lie on his back and stare upward for hours, plotting course headings in his mind, imagining the smooth feel of controls under his hands, and the jolting kick of power during a jump into hyperdrive. If he had a ship, he would take a trajectory off this planet straight up through the tail of the dragon, circle round the red-glowing planet that comprised its eye, and leave this system behind in his ion exhaust.

But tonight the stars were hidden by the dust, and he felt as though the ground were trying to engulf him. He'd certainly breathed enough of it today, and the smell of it lingered in his nostrils, beneath the stale scent of recycled air in the mask.

He was tired, feeling every one of his seventy years. The slow pacing made his recently healed legs ache. Gravity seemed very strong tonight.

Most of the time he felt like a fifth wheel. The colonists didn't need his skills, and about all he could find to do was go on scouting forays. They reminded him of his youth, when he'd been a belt pilot, picking up jobs where and when he could find them, flying old scrap heaps and junkers that could barely hold oxygen. He'd done some scouting for mining companies among the asteroid belts. Later had come the better jobs, the better ships, and finally his current position as a government pilot. He'd been in deep sleep more years than not, but here the only sleep came at night, and even it wasn't safe from—

"Solace?" came Danziger's gruff voice over his gear.

Alonzo blinked himself out of his thoughts quickly. "Yeah? Problem?"

"No. Morgan's going to spell you."

Alonzo frowned and checked the time. It was after

midnight. He'd lost track of the hours, as he so often did at night.

"Yeah, okay," he said reluctantly. He hated going in, but his body was screaming for rest. "Who's going to spell you?"

"Baines. In about an hour," Danziger replied. "Sleep well."

Yeah, Alonzo thought wryly, sleep while the buffaloes went by like ore freighters in a shipping yard. "Thanks," he said and went in.

The interior of the tent was quiet, with everyone bedded down except Devon. She was working on something by the dim glow of a solar lamp. On its lowest setting the little lamp could run off its stored power for hours. She glanced up as he came in, slapping dust off his clothing and pulling off the mask. Her brown eyes looked large and preoccupied; she was obviously busy.

Alonzo glanced around for Julia and saw her sleeping near the children. Her unbound hair spilled softly across the flat pillow; one pale tendril curled on her cheek. Seen like this, she was not the formidable doctor, but a beautiful woman. Some of his restless tension softened for a moment. His fingers itched to touch that curl of silky hair, to brush it gently from her face, but instead he made his way quietly over to a corner of unoccupied bunks and folded out one for himself.

In moments he was asleep.

"Starstrider."

The voice was a soft murmur, calling to him. Alonzo frowned.

"Starstrider, come."

He turned and saw the silhouette of a tall figure approaching him.

Alonzo's frown deepened with dismay. He realized he was in a cave, one that vaulted overhead with ribs of stone that made him feel as though he'd been swallowed by a whale. The air smelled earthy and damp. A cool, gentle breeze blew into his face. It stirred the garments of the Terrian walking toward him. Light shone in the distance, although he could see no source for it.

Alonzo tried to run from the Terrian, but his feet were mired. Glancing down, he saw himself buried in dirt to the knees. Try as he might, he could not pull free.

"Starstrider."

The voice remained soft, almost inflectionless.

Reluctantly Alonzo stopped fighting it and faced the Terrian, who now stood before him. Alonzo looked up into the alien's face and resigned himself. He had never understood why the aliens could only communicate with humans through dreams. He had never understood why they always sought him. He was just a pilot, stranded on G889 by the crash, an unwilling member of this expedition, and if he ever got the chance to go offworld again, he would probably sell his soul to do it.

"I am Solace," he said.

The Terrian gestured gracefully. "Names are seeds carried by the wind. Actions are roots that reach deep into the earth."

"Why have you come to me?" Alonzo asked. "What do you want?"

"There is much you seek, Starstrider. Much you do not find."

Alonzo hated talking in riddles. "We need water, if that's what you mean."

"You seek the lost place."

Suddenly Alonzo was interested. "You mean the mountains? You know where to find them? You can help us?"

"I come to give warning."

"Against what?" As he spoke, Alonzo thought of the Grendler who had already warned them against entering the valley. Now it made sense. The Grendler must have told the first Terrian band he encountered, and they had sought out the colonists.

"It is the time of passing. Much is unsettled. Much is to change."

"I don't understand," Alonzo said. "All we're trying to do is find water and be on our way."

"You seek the lost place. It is not to be found by those who do not walk in the way."

Alonzo thought of the items he'd picked up earlier; the skull, the staff, and the bone. He wished now he hadn't tampered with them. "We aren't trying to offend you or your way," he said carefully. "We aren't trying to intrude on anything that's sacred to you. But without water we'll die."

"The herds come. It is the time of passing."

"What is it, an annual migration?" Alonzo asked.

"As you say. Many animals come. This time is theirs. You have hunted. You have killed."

"Only to survive, only to protect ourselves."

"No one stands here at the time of passing. It is their time. They are not to be hunted."

"We are sorry for our mistake," Alonzo said, spreading out his hands. "We will not hunt them again."

The Terrian was silent for a while, towering over Alonzo, inscrutable in the dim light. "This is true in your heart."

"Yes."

"Mistakes are the way of a child."

"We are children here," Alonzo said, sweating. "Everything is new to us. We make many mistakes."

"To learn from mistakes is to grow."

"Yes."

"You wander far, like the Grendlers."

"We have far to go."

"Then take a different path. This one is closed. You have seen the taboo mark, but you did not understand it. Now you have learned."

"Why is the valley forbidden?" Alonzo asked.

The Terrian did not answer.

"All we want is water. If there's no water past the valley, we will take a different route. Will you show us where there's water?"

The Terrian did not answer.

"Water, for us, is like salt fruit for you," Alonzo said with a rising sense of desperation. "We must have it to drink or we'll die. If you don't have salt fruit, you'll die. Will you help us?"

"I have come in kindness, Starstrider, to warn you."

"And I'm grateful for your kindness," Alonzo said. "But—"

"If you will not learn, there is no more to be said."

"But why can't we cross the valley?" Alonzo asked. "You came to help us; why won't you tell—"

"You can enter the valley," the Terrian said sternly.

"Well, then—"

"But when you have done the forbidden, leaving is not an easy thing."

Alonzo swallowed. "We don't want to offend you. Tell us what to do."

"Choose another path."

"Which one?" he asked in exasperation. "North or south? How far does the valley extend? How far will we have to go—"

The Terrian turned abruptly and walked away.

Alonzo tried to go after him, but his feet were still trapped in the soil. "Wait!" he called. "Wait! I don't understand . . ."

But the Terrian never glanced back, and Alonzo awoke abruptly, trembling from a cold sweat.

He looked around, wiping his hand across his damp face, and realized he could see through the gray light inside the tent. Dawn light, very cold and still.

Groaning softly to himself, he sat up and swung his legs off the bunk. He propped his aching head in his hands. Why did the Terrians have to make things so difficult? Why couldn't they just come right out and say what they meant?

"Alonzo?" came Julia's voice, very quiet.

He looked up and swiftly sat on his hands to hide their trembling.

She walked over to him, her face still puffy from sleep, her hair not yet pinned up for the day. He wished she would always wear her hair loose and flowing like this, but he didn't tell her so.

"Something wrong?" she asked. "Bad dream?"

He nodded, irked by her sharp observation. While he had come to respect her skill as a doctor and was grateful to her for healing his legs, he still wasn't used to being watched so closely, or of having to answer to others.

He'd always been a loner, a party man for the hour, then gone, off to the next job, the next adventure, unfettered. He knew women in every port, women who pined for his return, women who aged while deep sleep kept him young.

Yet here he was forced to interact with the members of the group. He admired Devon; she was a good leader. He liked Danziger, who left people alone when they wanted it. And there was Julia, whom he'd disliked at first and now found himself watching too often, thinking about too much. Another cage, if he chose to stick his neck into it.

He frowned and stood up, brushing off her concern. "It's quiet outside. Did the herd finally go by?"

"Yes. You want some of Bess's coffee? There isn't much. The tank is leaking again."

His head whipped around. He met her eyes and saw his own worry reflected in hers. "Damn," he said softly.

"Alonzo," she said hesitantly, "did you dream?"

He knew what she was asking. He knew she could tell. Reluctantly he nodded.

At once Julia stepped back. "Devon's outside, if you have something to tell her."

He wished he didn't. They were in a fix, all right, and what he had to relate wasn't going to help matters.

"Thanks," he said and walked outside to do it.

Chapter 5

• • • • • • • ● ●

Devon stood alone at the edge, gazing down into the sharp cut of the valley. The eastern sun glowed orange behind her, spreading an eerie light through the dusty fog and filling the valley with strange shadows. The ground had stopped shaking an hour ago. The deafening rumble had faded with the passing of the main herd. Now only a few stragglers still trotted by, half-seen through the dust, their shaggy bodies ghostly in this light.

Devon lifted her chin. Her eyes were gritty from dust and insufficient sleep. Her muscles ached from yesterday's exertions. But all she felt was determination to cross that valley and find water.

The patch on the tank had failed in the night despite Danziger's efforts to save it. Now each of them had only a full canteen, and there were a few bottles stowed in the cargo hold of the TransRover.

A chilly wind swept across her back. She heard it sigh down the slope into the bottom of the valley, rustling through the few weeds still standing on the churned ground. Across the valley, atop the distant cliffs, a scavenger howled and was answered by a chorus of yips. The primeval sound made Devon shiver, and her uneasiness returned. The scavengers would naturally follow the herd to pick on weak or injured animals. Devon knew she had nothing to fear from the scavengers. They were vicious but timid, and scattered at any sight of humans.

Still, for some reason she felt reluctant to descend. She wasn't sure why. The Grendler's warning hadn't convinced her of any specific danger. And yet she couldn't help but think of the blackened skull back there in the road as a warning beacon.

Warning against what?

And when had Terrians or Grendlers built roads? The Terrians were a tribal society, living underground. The Grendlers were wanderers, seldom seen in groups. Neither had need of roads.

Devon gave her thoughts a shake. She wasn't here to solve ancient mysteries. They'd better get started.

She turned and saw Alonzo's tall, straight figure walking through the orange-tinted dust. When he reached her, she saw that his eyes were red and his black hair rumpled as though he hadn't bothered to comb it. Usually he flashed her a brilliant grin or winked in greeting, the deviltry evident in his gaze, but this morning he looked subdued, even somber.

She frowned. "What is it?"

He sighed and said without preamble, "A Terrian contacted me."

"In a dream?"

He nodded.

Devon's frown deepened. "What about?"

"Our being here. Our plans."

"To cross the valley?"

He nodded again. "It's forbidden."

"Great." Anger filled her throat. She threw out her hands. "First the Grendler and now the Terrians. What's so special about this dust bowl?"

"He wouldn't say." Alonzo grimaced and rolled his eyes. "You know how they are. Riddles in every word."

"So what did he tell you?" she demanded.

"First, the herds are sacred or something while they're migrating. The Terrians are steamed that we killed one. No one's supposed to be out here during the migrations."

"No kidding," Devon said dryly. "Reason one being it's a very good way to get run over."

A ghost of a grin flickered across Alonzo's handsome face. "They're also mad because we're looking for what he called the lost place."

Devon was startled. "The mountains that don't exist? How would they know about that?"

Alonzo shrugged. "He never said anything about mountains. This valley is forbidden and he wants us to go another way."

"Did you ask him about water?"

"Of course, but he said *nada*. I tried every way I could to explain our situation to him, but he wasn't having it. We've stumbled onto a sacred place or something, and it's taboo for us to enter."

"Did he say what would happen if we don't respect the taboo?"

"No. Just gave me a warning. He was pretty tight-lipped about the whole subject." Alonzo's face twisted in frustration. "Why do they bother to contact us if they aren't going to say things straight out?"

"They're not like us," Devon said, feeling that she was stating the obvious. "Maybe they think they are being clear."

Alonzo frowned worriedly. "Julia says the tank's leaking again."

She nodded, staring at the valley. "There's water beyond those cliffs. Your sensors picked it up."

"Yeah."

"When you were scouting yesterday, did you find any more taboo markers along this side of the valley?"

"Nope. And I know what you're going to ask next. Could we go farther along this edge before we descend?"

She smiled, amused by how he loved to show off.

He shook his head. "We've got a fairly easy slope at this point, but if we go south this side gets steeper until we have cliffs. If we go north, same thing. This is the way in."

"And on the other side?" she asked softly in disappointment.

"The cliffs run a long way to the north. I didn't track that very far. But if we go south about ten klicks or so, the valley starts to broaden out."

"So we go in at this point and follow it until we can climb out."

"Yep, and down that way is where I got the reading for water. We may have to dig for it. It wasn't a surface reading. I'd want to scan again to verify its location and availability."

She kept her face wooden, accepting what he said without emotion. After a certain point, with setbacks falling one right after the other, she had no more worry left in her to go around.

"I've always tried to respect the Terrians," she said after a moment of silence.

"Yes."

"But we don't have a choice. Whatever significance this valley has for them, we have to ignore it this time."

Alonzo nodded, although he didn't look eager. "You're right. I don't see another way."

Danziger appeared in the gloom, his dark bulk a reassuring silhouette. "I've got the tent folded down, and all the cargo's loaded," he reported. Like the rest of them, he looked bleary-eyed and tired. He scratched his beard stubble and yawned. "Everyone's ready."

Alonzo said, "I was also told the valley is easy to enter but hard to leave. I don't know what that means."

Uneasiness returned to Devon, but she brushed it aside. "I guess we'll find out on the way. Let's go."

The eastern slope was not sheer like the western side, but it was steeper than it looked, and tricky work to get the vehicles down. The ATV zigzagged easily, but the TransRover lurched and staggered, swaying heavily from side to side as it crept cautiously down the vestige of road. Partway down, the road vanished altogether, but Danziger kept working the TransRover down by cautious degrees, angling at first, then doing switchbacks as necessary.

He allowed no passengers in the TransRover's cab this morning, fearing injuries if he overturned. Everyone on foot followed the vehicles, making sure they stayed out of the way in case of mishap.

But finally all three vehicles were down, and they idled until the rest of the group caught up.

The sun wasn't high enough yet to reach into the bottom of the valley. Gloomy shadows made the scant vegetation look purple. The ground had been heavily torn by hooves. Here and there fresh piles of manure steamed in the cold air. In the distance northward they could hear a lone bellow, but even the rumble of the migrating herd was fading away.

The colonists huddled together, slowly sorting themselves into a column between the DuneRail and the Trans-Rover.

Morgan was still grumbling. "Now we're down," he said to Bess. "How are we supposed to get out? Strap on anti-gravs and fly? Look over there. It's straight up as far as the eye can see."

Ignoring him, Devon climbed back into the ATV. She glanced at the DuneRail, where Alonzo and Julia were sharing the seat.

"Scanners on," Alonzo reported.

Devon nodded. "Okay," she said grimly. "Let's go south and look for water."

But it was True who yelled, "Look! Everybody, look!"

Across the valley, the first strong rays of sunlight were striking the western cliff face. There had been a landslide in the night, and the sun was glinting off something pale and smooth revealed by the fallen rock.

Alonzo squinted. "What is that?"

Devon stood up on the seat and stared. Like a spotlight, the sunshine continued to spread across the cliff, illuminating a yawning cavity that had not been visible yesterday. And flanking that opening were white columns of stone, columns polished and carved.

"It's . . ." She paused, swallowing, her disbelief warring with the evidence before her. "It looks like a gateway."

"Impossible," Julia said.

"But it's *there*," True said. "Let's go and look at it."

Devon slowly climbed down behind the ATV's controls. She still couldn't believe it. Nothing she'd encountered thus far of the Terrian and Grendler cultures indicated they were capable of something like this. But then she reminded herself that very little about G889 had turned out as expected. It wasn't even supposed to have sentient life forms, yet it did. Now this.

She swept the ATV's sensor array at the gateway. The sensors confirmed what everyone was seeing. Opening the storage bin, she pulled out a pair of jumpers and lifted them for a better look.

A bounce on the seat beside her jarred her.

"Sorry," True said. "Can I look too, please? I saw it first."

"Okay," Devon said, unable to resist the excitement in True's eyes. "Hang on a sec."

She adjusted the jumpers and scanned the cliffs. The columns were carved full length with intricate alien designs unlike anything she'd ever seen. They stood well back beneath an overhang in the cliff face, and only this particular angle of sunlight made them visible. The cavern yawning beyond them looked large and quite dark.

Still feeling stunned, Devon lowered the jumpers and handed them to True.

"Is it a Terrian place?" Julia asked her.

Devon shrugged. "I don't know. I haven't seen anything like it before."

Her eyes hurt, and she rubbed them.

"Wow," True said softly. "That white stone really reflects the light. It almost hurts to look at it."

Uly came running up. "What is it?" he asked. "What's going on? Can I see?"

True handed him the jumpers, scooting over to make room for him on the seat. She tilted her head to look at Devon from beneath the brim of her cap. "We have to go look at it," she said. "Please, Devon. Can't we explore just a little?"

No go, the Grendler had said. *The valley is forbidden,* the Terrian had said.

Devon pushed the warnings from her mind. "How can we ignore it?" she said.

True squealed. "Great! Let's go! Let's go!"

"Devon," Alonzo said, "I'm showing a water trace in that direction, probably in the rock itself, but—"

Hope rekindled in Devon. "Let's check it out," she said and gunned the ATV.

As they drew closer they saw that what had appeared to be a landslide was actually a ramp of sorts leading up the cliff to the gateway. It had been cleverly constructed to appear in the distance like a natural fall. Rough stone abutments of natural rock face projected out at angles on either side of the gateway, again serving to conceal the overhang and cavern, especially from anyone standing on top of the eastern slope, as they had yesterday.

Everyone halted at the foot of the ramp. Close up, they could see that it was a massive construction of intricately laid stone. No mortar had been used; it had been entirely dry laid, yet it was solid, and snugged against the base of the cliffs with the outside rim curved and bumped out irregularly to make it seem natural from a distance.

Devon waited until Danziger parked the TransRover at the base of the ramp, which was wide enough even for that massive piece of machinery. When Danziger climbed down from the cab, she said, "Let's go up and look."

"I want to go," True said.

"Me too!" piped Uly.

Devon shook her head at the children. "Not yet. Let us check it out first."

Their faces twisted with disappointment.

"I found it," True said.

Danziger looked at his daughter in annoyance. "You know the rules."

True frowned and kicked the ground, but made no further protest.

Uly gave his mother his best sad-eyed look of appeal, which she ignored with a hidden smile.

Devon started up the ramp, Danziger following with his rifle unslung and ready.

Alonzo dropped Julia off and drove the DuneRail on down the valley for further exploration, as restless as an eagle sailing the sky. The others perched themselves on stones to wait.

"Don't take long," Morgan called out to Devon. "We have to find water, remember."

In reply she waved the hand scanner she carried and kept going.

At this angle they couldn't see the gateway, yet the ramp itself was a marvel.

"This is amazing," Devon kept repeating. "Who made this? When? How?"

"Why did they go to so much trouble to hide it?" Danziger replied.

"Precise natural camouflage, using the principles of perspective to fool the naked eye," Devon said, her head swiveling as she took in everything.

They reached the top of the ramp and found themselves at the far edge of the overhang. Set in deep beneath it were the white columns, with the cavern mouth beyond.

Danziger tilted back his head and walked into the shade. "Big," he muttered.

The space was enormous. Nothing had prepared Devon for the size and proportion of this landing. They could have parked three TransRovers beneath the overhang.

From the ground below, the abutments had looked like natural projections of stone. She saw now that they had been carefully carved to look that way. She put out her hand and touched the rough surface. This close, she could clearly see the chisel marks, worn by age but still deep.

Alonzo reported in over his gear: "I'm about three hundred meters down the valley. The ramp and cavern aren't visible from where I am, especially since the sun's getting higher. Weird."

Devon and Danziger exchanged glances. "Then if we hadn't been down in the valley floor at precisely the right time," Devon began. "At precisely the right spot—"

"True wouldn't have seen it," Danziger said. "None of us would."

Devon shook her head, still amazed. She activated the scanner and swept it slowly around in a 180-degree circle. "The rock walls show stability. And the water indication is definite."

She aimed the scanner straight at the gateway. "We have a large system of caves."

Danziger sighed. "Typical Terrian high rise."

Devon grinned to herself. "With a structural mass inside. The readings aren't clear about what that is, but it's quite large. Stone or—wait. Maybe that's what the probe registered. They're sensitive. And with this thing large and close to the surface, it could have shown up as—"

"Devon, listen. If we've found a Terrian place, then let's get our water and leave," Danziger said. "Every time we encounter the Terrians we wind up in complications we're better off without."

She shook her head, unwilling to rush. "I'm not getting any life forms, nothing human-sized. And the water analysis shows drinkable elements."

Tremendous relief rolled over her. For a moment she felt almost dizzy. "Thank God," she said with feeling. "I thought we were done for."

"No, you didn't," Danziger said gruffly, but his eyes were

kind. "You weren't going to give up until you drove us on our hands and knees to get to wherever we had to. Looks like we've lucked out."

She nodded, hoping it was luck. Hoping things had turned for a while and would go their way now.

"So we get the water and hurry out of here," Danziger said.

"No Terrians are around right now," she said. "I think it's okay. We need the rest."

"Yeah," he agreed, squinting down the ramp to the TransRover. He frowned. "We're running on borrowed time with most of this equipment. A lot of things need repairs, and we can't store water until I fix the tanks. Rewelding those seams is really a shop job, but I think I can manage."

"Of course you can," she said.

He sent her a sharp look. "Don't make me into a hero," he said gruffly. "I'm a good mechanic, but I don't work miracles. Don't ever start thinking we're invincible on my end."

She frowned, taken aback by his rebuke. "Okay," she said meekly. "How much time will you need?"

"It's hard to say, several hours at best," he said, still frowning. "Maybe by the time you actually locate the water in those caves, I'll be ready to give you a firm estimate."

She nodded.

Giving her one last stern look, he slung his rifle over his shoulder and started down the ramp.

Devon activated her gear. "True, could you bring the other scanner up here and give a hand?"

"Be there on the double," True said at once.

Devon smiled to herself.

In less than a minute the kids were running up the ramp, passing Danziger on the way. Via gear, Devon informed the others of their findings and suggested they set up camp at the base of the ramp.

Uly came hurrying up to Devon, his wavy brown hair blowing back off his forehead. "This is incredible!" he shouted, making his voice echo off the stones. "Look at it! Hey, Mom, listen."

He cupped his hands to his mouth and shouted again. The echoes reverberated around them.

Devon glanced up at the overhang of granite over the gateway. "Okay, enough. We don't want to shake this rock down on our heads."

Uly, however, was already swinging around her. He ran to one of the white columns and climbed up on its base, then jumped down and ran toward the darkness yawning beyond.

"Uly, stop!" Devon called in alarm.

Reluctantly he halted and glanced over his shoulder with a grimace. "Aw, Mom. We gotta see what's in there."

"Don't be juvenile," True told him loftily. "It has to be checked out with scanners first. Isn't the one you have working?"

Devon slipped it into her pocket. "A little fuzzy on the readouts. Probably dust in the casing."

True nodded. "I can clean it out later if you want. That is, if Dad doesn't need me to help him."

"I'm sure he will, but meanwhile why don't you run some checks for me? We might as well be doubly sure of our data."

"Okay."

Chestnut hair swinging around her jawline, True grinned at Devon from beneath the bill of her cap and headed toward the cave mouth.

"Stay in the gate and do a slow sweep," Devon told her. "Don't go in until I tell you."

"Check," True said. Uly darted after her.

Keeping a wary eye on her impulsive son, Devon pulled out her hand computer and started tapping in a quick log entry. She heard others coming up the ramp.

"It's so big!" Uly kept saying. He ran to the edge of the ramp and called down, "Hey, Yale, you gotta see this! Come on!"

When the tutor finally reached the top, he stopped just as the others had and moved in a slow, awestruck circle. "It has something of the aspect of the ancient Egyptian and Mesopotamian architectural styles," Yale announced. "The builders had an advanced understanding of perspective and proportion. These carvings show a deep appreciation of aesthetics. Uly, look at that friezework extending into the cave. The ancient Greeks used to carve friezes, showing battle scenes as well as tableaux of their mythological figures. Perhaps this was used for a similar function."

Bess was standing out near the edge as though she didn't want to be under the overhang. Her eyes were wide. "This has been here a really long time."

"The scanner says between two and three thousand years," True called out.

"Fabulous," Devon murmured. She pointed at the top of the columns. "Look at the carving. The detail is still perfect, hardly worn at all."

"It's protected back in under there," Julia said. She walked over to the gateway to stand by True. "I brought a torch. Are we ready to go inside?"

"No animals living inside," True reported from her scanner readings. "Walls are stable. The cave ceiling is stable. It won't fall in on us. Yeah, Devon, can we go inside now?"

Devon smiled at her, admiring her energy. "Better ask your dad."

True was on her gear immediately. "Dad, Devon and Julia

are about to go inside the cave. Can I . . . But, Dad, I really . . . Oh, okay. Yeah, I guess so."

She sighed, every line of her slim, straight body sagging dejectedly. "He's about to take off the fuel feed line and he needs me to hold the wrenches."

Grimacing, she snapped off her scanner and handed it to Julia. "That's not a critical repair. He could wait on it for a while," she grumbled.

Normally True was eager to help her father work on the equipment. But could any kid ever resist the lure of a cave? Devon and Julia exchanged glances. Devon could feel her own excitement stirring. She couldn't wait to see the other wonders beyond the gate.

"You better get going," Devon prodded the girl.

True yanked off her cap and slapped it against her leg. "I guess so." She saw Uly grinning at her and stiffened. "He isn't going with you, is he? Because that's not fair—"

"No, Uly's not going," Devon said.

A frown creased Uly's face. "Aw, Mom!"

"No, you have lessons to do."

"But I—"

"No arguments, young man," Devon said sternly. Over Uly's head, she met Yale's eyes. The old man gave her a tiny nod of complete accord. She patted her son's shoulder. "You can go in later, if there's anything to see. You and True together, okay?"

He sighed, not too interested in her promise, although she knew he'd pester her about it later. "Okay," he finally said.

"I'm coming too," Morgan said suddenly. He pulled a torch from his pocket and swung the beam about impatiently. "I think this place has possibilities."

He didn't say what kind of possibilities, and Devon didn't ask. Morgan was always working on an angle. Besides, she still hadn't forgiven him for offering to trade Bess's mini-hologram to the Grendler. She hoped Bess had the thing back in her own possession, because it wasn't safe with Morgan.

Torches shining on low beam, they moved cautiously through the vast gateway.

The darkness seemed to swallow them immediately. But the natural light shining in from their backs helped light the way somewhat.

Devon inhaled cool, dry air. It smelled slightly musty, and she expected that scent to intensify as they walked farther into the interior.

The cave's roof vaulted high overhead. There was no sense of confinement. Halfway up the wall ran the decorative frieze carved into the granite itself. Many of the forms and figures were unrecognizable, almost abstract shapes. But as they advanced slowly, the carving began to look more familiar: flowers and vines, then elongated Terrian figures kneeling in supplication before a mythological beast that was partly animal and partly a disk with radiating lines extending from it.

"Some kind of sun god?" Devon suggested.

"Look," Julia said, pointing at the opposite wall. "There are more symbols, many of them the same."

The sun disk appeared often from that point until the frieze stopped completely. In the center of the wall at that point, however, a gigantic sun disk had been carved. It was taller than a Terrian in height, dwarfing the humans. Morgan walked up to it and cautiously touched one of the radiant lines with his fingertips.

"Sun god mythology is common to many cultures," Devon said, wishing they'd brought Yale along to make more comparisons. "Why not here?"

Morgan snorted skeptically. "Sun worship from tribes who live underground?"

"Okay," Devon said, feeling a little defensive. "It's just a theory. Maybe the Terrians didn't always live underground."

"Or maybe they worshipped the two moons," Julia suggested. "Look."

She shone her torch past the sun disk to reveal a wide, arched doorway. Two stone animals stood on their hind feet, and where their front paws joined, an archway was formed. On the wall to the left, a pair of crescent moons had been carved, fully as large as the sun disk.

"This is incredible," Devon whispered. "Julia, are you recording any of this on your vid feed?"

"Sure am," the doctor replied excitedly. "I never dreamed the Terrians had anything like this in their past."

"Why, because they're so backward now?" Morgan asked.

Devon frowned. "They aren't backward. You can't make simple judgments like that."

"They lack civilization," he said impatiently. "They have no cities, no structure beyond a rudimentary tribal organization. They live in caves like animals and they have simple, agrarian lives. Anyone could overrun this planet and take it away from them just like that." He snapped his fingers. "Which is exactly what we're doing."

"We are not overrunning them," Devon argued.

"Oh, please. Let's not kid ourselves," he said. "We're here, aren't we? They were here first, but we aren't leaving."

"We can't leave," Julia muttered.

"No excuse. We staked this out, and we're keeping it."

"There's plenty of room for all of us," Devon said.

"Yeah, and according to history that's what other tribal types in Earth's past were promised, but it's not what they got."

Julia eyed him in surprise. "I thought you were pro-colonization. Since when did you start defending the Terrians?"

"Who's defending them?" Morgan said. "Not me. I'm just pointing out facts. As soon as we get established, these primitives will be—"

"The Terrians aren't exactly primitive," Devon said. "Those lightning sticks and the dreams—"

"Yeah, but that's all mystical stuff," Morgan broke in impatiently. "They can't build a TransRover. They can't manufacture a star drive. They can't conceive of a space station, let alone—"

"Achievements run in many different directions," Devon said, rendered uncomfortable by what he was saying. Morgan was trying to say they were superior to the Terrians just because they possessed advanced technology. Devon didn't subscribe to that view. "We barely know what the Terrians are capable of. It's going to take time and patience to turn them into our allies. Eventually we may learn some of their secrets."

Morgan snorted. "I'm telling you, history repeats itself. The Terrians don't stand a chance against progress."

Anger flared in Devon. "I didn't bring this colony to G889 to destroy what's already here. We will establish a peaceful coexistence with the Terrians. I'm determined to make that happen."

"It's a naive view, but, okay, you're entitled to it," he said, holding up his hands. "Just don't say I didn't warn you."

Julia frowned at him. "Exactly what are you trying to warn us against? I get the feeling there's a hidden agenda here."

He blinked and assumed a bland expression. "No way. You're wrong."

"Well, anyway," Devon said, refusing to let Morgan

disturb her, "finding this is going to help us understand the Terrians better."

"How?" Morgan asked. "It's just old stone carvings and mumbo jumbo."

"You were saying we can learn from the past," Julia reminded him with an arched eyebrow.

"Oh. Oh, yeah." He grinned sheepishly and avoided their gazes.

Devon took a directional bearing on her scanner as a safety precaution, although there hadn't been any branching passageways so far. Then, shining her torch ahead, she stepped through the sun-and-moon archway.

The path ahead of her suddenly lit up with thousands of tiny pinpoints of sparkling light.

Startled, Devon jumped back, bumping into Julia. "Sorry," she said breathlessly. "What's going on?"

Morgan's torchlight crisscrossed with Devon's, stabbing back and forth along floor and walls. Everywhere their torchlight touched, the tiny bits of light began to glitter.

"Whatever it is, we're causing it," Morgan said.

"Activating it," Julia corrected. Scanner in hand, she crouched low and took some readings. "Here, look at this."

Devon joined her and saw that the light source was coming from what looked like little bits of rock. She stretched out her hand but didn't touch.

"What is it?"

"It looks something like coral. It's a living plant organism," Julia said, still reading off her scanner. "Something in its chemical makeup is highly reflective. When you shine light on it, it releases a chemical that's somehow generating a quasi light source. Kind of like phosphorus on an old stump in the woods. That's not a very technical explanation, but—"

"We don't need a botany lecture," Morgan interrupted. "Let's go on."

Devon glanced at Julia. "Will it damage the coral if we walk on it?"

"Only if you step on the dead areas. That's brittle, and our weight will probably crush it. But anything that shines light should be fairly resilient."

Rising to her feet, Devon stepped cautiously across the tiny coral, shining her torch with care. Morgan trampled past her without heed. "Come on," he said impatiently. "I'm beginning to have some theories about this place."

She glared at his back, but followed more quickly, with Julia bringing up the rear. The coral field was narrow and less than forty meters in length before they came to what appeared to be a dead end.

Devon stared at it in frustration. "We have to find a way to that water. These caves don't end here. There's much more beyond, according to my scanner."

Julia sighed and looked back the way they'd come. Already the coral field was beginning to dim back to darkness. "Maybe there's another archway. We could have taken the wrong turn."

Morgan spun on his heel immediately. "I'll go check."

"We should stay together," Devon said.

"Why?"

Both women just looked at him.

Morgan frowned. "Look, I think this is an old temple of some kind."

"Obviously," Julia murmured.

"Yeah, and so there're probably some burial chambers and altars. Old temples used to have storehouses, places to put the offerings and such."

"Is there a point to this?" Devon asked.

He looked at her as if she were stupid. "Treasure. Bound to be here."

She couldn't believe him. "The only treasure we're looking for is the liquid kind. We can't go off on a wild-goose chase like that."

"Why not? What's wrong with making the best of an opportunity?"

Devon shook her head. "I'm not even going to get into this." Something was tickling the back of her mind. Frowning, she said, "This whole place is built on illusion, right?"

"What are you getting at?" Julia asked. "You think that the next gateway is concealed somehow?"

"Obviously," Morgan said. "Or we took the wrong—"

"Let me try something," Devon broke in. She stepped forward, holding her hand out before her. Her torch activated the coral growing on the stone wall blocking her path. She noticed that the coral didn't grow in one circular pattern. Devon touched the stone, running her fingers along its surface. Halfway across, she touched a fissure. Stepping closer, she discovered that the rock was cut at a sharp angle and she could squeeze sideways through the passage.

"I found it," she said excitedly. "Come on!"

Without waiting for the others, she pushed her way along the stone. It was worn very smooth in this narrow space. For a moment she almost felt as though the rock were pushing back, trying to crush her, then she was through the passageway and her momentary claustrophobia was gone and forgotten.

She found herself standing on a narrow ledge high above an enormous cavern, a seemingly endless cavern, much larger than what her torch could illuminate. Spreading below her was a city made of white stone that reflected her torchlight brilliantly. She stared at walls, spiraling staircases, arched windows, and short towers with domed tops, some with narrow bridges spanning the distance between them. There were buildings of every size and description, set along narrow streets designed for foot traffic. High above, in the great domed ceiling of the cavern, a narrow fissure opened to the sky, and sunlight spilled down in a tight beam of magical light. It bathed the tallest tower at the center of this small city, turning the white stone golden for a few moments.

In the distance Devon could hear the sweet, wonderful sound of running water. She closed her eyes a moment and inhaled, imagining she could smell it as well.

"Devon?" Julia called from behind her. "Where did you go? Devon!"

Devon turned her head fractionally, unable to take her eyes completely off the sight. "Come on!" she called back. "You won't believe this."

Only then did Julia come through the diagonal passageway. She stumbled onto the ledge, almost tripping over Devon, and gasped as she took in the sight before them.

"My God," she whispered.

"This is ridiculous," Morgan grumbled, joining them. "Hardly enough room to . . ." His voice trailed off as though it had failed him completely. He stared, his mouth hanging open.

"Isn't it beautiful?" Devon said. She snapped off her torch and crouched on her haunches, content simply to look.

"It's magnificent," Julia whispered. "The last thing I expected. The architecture is so beautiful, it's almost holy—"

"Exactly," Morgan broke in eagerly. "I told you this was a temple of some kind. Now we find a whole little city, probably full of temples . . . and treasure."

"Morgan, the city itself is the treasure," Devon said, but he wasn't listening.

He stepped past her and hurried on, following the ledge as it angled down the wall toward the ground below.

"Morgan—" Devon began, but he paid her no attention.

She looked at Julia and sighed. "I guess he's going to be too busy to help us now."

"Looks like it." Julia didn't seem to mind. "I hear running water."

"Yes." Devon switched on her scanner. "Over there, this side of the city walls."

They started down the ledge, taking more care with the uneven footing than Morgan had. But before they reached the bottom, Danziger was calling over Devon's gear, his voice tight with urgency.

"Devon, we've got trouble. Devon!"

"I'm here," she answered at once. "What is it?"

Her mind was suddenly full of angry Terrians, swarming to defend their holy city. "Danziger!" she called. "Come in. I'm not reading you now."

The mechanic didn't answer.

Alarm spread through Devon. "Danziger," she called. "John! Answer me!"

But there was only static in response.

Chapter 6

• • • • • • • ●

Devon went pounding back across the magical coral, back through the archway, back beneath the mythological carvings of the friezework, and burst out through the gateway into the dazzling sunlight just in time to be almost run over by the ATV.

The red vehicle lurched to a halt, half throwing Bess against the controls. She stared at Devon, who stared back, frozen, her heart still pounding from how close she'd come to being hit.

Bess recovered first and glanced over her shoulder before gesturing Devon out of the way. Devon backed up, and Bess drove the ATV on to park it against the stone abutment near the gateway. Strained engine roar came from the ramp up to the cavern, and only then did Devon register other sounds, among them a distant rumble that made her heart sink.

"Not again!" she cried.

Bess climbed out of the ATV and came running. "Are you okay?" she demanded, gripping Devon by the arms. "God, I thought I hit you."

"I'm fine," Devon said. "What—"

Bess hugged her tightly, then broke away. "They're coming," she said breathlessly. "Another herd. Alonzo called in and said it's nearly as big as the last one."

"Oh, no!" Julia said, emerging from the cave in time to hear. She stumbled to a halt and leaned over slightly to catch her breath. "I thought we'd seen enough buffalo for a lifetime yesterday."

"The migration," Devon said grimly. "We can't say we weren't warned."

At least the Terrian warning had turned out to have practical reasons behind it, rather than something mystical.

The TransRover engine revved higher, obviously laboring. Devon took a few steps toward the ramp, then scurried back out of concern of getting in Danziger's way.

She glanced overhead, wondering if there really was enough room. It was certainly spacious under the overhang, but still . . .

Then the TransRover's cab came into view, rising slowly into sight as it strained to make the incline. The gigantic wheels rolled ponderously, seemed almost to pause, then they grabbed and the TransRover came roaring in under the overhang. Only then did Devon see that Zero was behind the vehicle, pushing it up and over the final steepness of the grade.

The stone around them reverberated with engine noise so loud it rivaled the bawling, thundering herd coming fast. Parking the TransRover, Danziger shut off the engine, which whined with a protesting squeal Devon hadn't heard before.

Zero was pumping his arms in the way Uly had taught him. "Yes!" he shouted. "I knew we would get the Trans-Rover to the top. I can push any—"

"Yeah, Zero, thanks," Danziger said absently as he climbed down from the cab. Pushing past the robot, he immediately opened one of the engine panels. Quickly he disconnected something, and dark fluid jetted across his hands, burning him.

He jumped back with a shout, shaking his hands, and Julia hurried to him.

"Get back," he yelled and hurried to throw open the next engine panel and repeat the process. Again fluid spewed, splattering everywhere, then the pressure in the line was lost, and the spewing stopped.

Stepping back, Danziger took a rag and gingerly wiped the hot fluid from his hands, grimacing with pain.

True jumped down from the cab and ran to him. She looked appalled. "I did what you said. I shut off the pressure as soon as—"

"It's okay, baby," he said, soothing her.

But her mouth was clamped tight, and her bottom lip quivered. "It's not all right. I didn't shut off the valve in time. You're burned."

"I'll be fine. It's not bad."

Devon reached him then while Julia ran for her medikit. "Is it serious?" Devon asked.

He shook his head, wincing, and tossed the rag back in the tool bin. His gaze turned south, and Devon involuntarily turned with him.

She saw the cloud of dust rising into the air, saw the line of buffaloes approaching like a gray wall. The yellow DuneRail raced ahead of the oncoming animals. Devon's heart clutched with alarm, and Julia came up to them with a gasp.

"Oh, God," she breathed. "Alonzo's still out there."

"He'll make it," True said.

"Sure he will," Devon agreed.

But Danziger was frowning, his gaze never wavering from the DuneRail as it flew along.

"I never got to that cracked panel," Danziger muttered.

"It'll hold, Dad," True said, forcing confidence no one felt. "It has to hold."

From the corner of her eye Devon saw Danziger grimace with impatience, but he didn't say anything to True about the futility of depending on false hopes.

Devon held her breath. Right now they needed a lot of hope, and prayer.

Bess provided the latter, her eyes closed.

By now everyone else had made it up the ramp with the last of their belongings. Uly hopped on one foot, then the other. Yale stood gravely at the top of the ramp with his hands clasped at his back. Baines and Walman were grumbling between themselves.

"I had just gotten a good start on detaching the fluid lines in the TransRover for an overhaul when Alonzo gave the alarm," Danziger said to Devon.

Julia cleaned his hands and smeared salve across the burns, her touch deft but gentle, her gaze straying out to the valley again and again.

"He should stay put," she muttered angrily. "He's always out roaming. Why can't he stay where he belongs?"

"If he hadn't gone scouting," Danziger said in a gentle voice, "we'd have had insufficient warning. As it is, I barely got the essential connections jury-rigged back in place."

Julia bent over her work and said nothing.

From this angle it looked as if the herd were gaining on the DuneRail. Holding her breath, Devon gripped Uly by the shoulders and held onto him. For once he didn't squirm in protest.

"Is he going to make it, Mom?" he whispered.

She didn't answer, biting her lip in worry.

"He has to make it," Julia said fiercely. "Damn him! After all the work I did to heal those legs, I'll—"

She broke off, her voice ragged.

The DuneRail was close enough now for them to see Alonzo at the controls. The vehicle hit a stone, and bounced dangerously. For a second it looked as if it would tip over, but the pilot held it together, righted it, and sent it speeding on. But it had cost him precious seconds.

Devon tensed, her fingers digging into Uly's shoulders. "Come on. Come on," she whispered over and over, urging Alonzo on with all her will.

With a bellow, one of the herd leaders charged the DuneRail and butted it hard. The vehicle lurched and nearly spun out of control, then Alonzo righted it again. He sent it surging up the ramp, but the buffalo followed, bellowing with rage. The bull butted the DuneRail again, nearly knocking it off the ramp. Wheels spinning gravel, Alonzo held on as the back end slewed dangerously, then he was gunning it up and over the top. The buffalo came charging right after him into their midst.

People screamed and scattered. Devon yanked Uly and True out of the way, shoving them against the wall for safety, and Zero lumbered forward to help.

Danziger, however, was already lifting his rifle. "Zero, freeze!" he ordered to keep the robot out of his line of fire.

Zero stopped in his tracks.

Danziger fired, and with a final bellow the bull toppled in mid-stride and crashed to the ground.

Suddenly it was over. Devon blinked and straightened from where she had been clutching Uly and True. Both children were wide-eyed and quiet. Devon gulped in a breath.

Danziger stood over the bull grimly, his rifle still aimed in case any more buffalo decided to come up the ramp.

"Wow," Uly said softly. "It almost got us."

"It would have, except for Dad," True said. Her eyes shone in her father's direction. The koba still clung firmly to her shoulder, its beady eyes equally bright.

"He's pretty cool," Uly told her. "Someday I'm going to be able to shoot like that. We'll go on safaris and bring back—"

Devon stepped away from them and went to Alonzo, who was standing next to the DuneRail, obviously shaken but still able to smile. He offered his hand to Danziger, who shook his gingerly, with a wince.

"Thanks," Alonzo said. "That was a little close."

"You think any more of them will come up here?" Devon asked.

Danziger shook his head. "Probably not. If one strays, though, others will probably follow. We'd better set a guard. Baines, you want to handle it?"

"Uh, sure," the crewman said and unslung his rifle.

Alonzo wiped the sweat off his forehead and drank from his canteen. His hands were unsteady, and he had some trouble getting the cap back on. He smiled, though, and gave Julia a wink. She went on frowning at him.

"Hey," he said. "I made it. Relax."

"You take too many risks," she said, and walked away briskly.

Alonzo watched her a moment, then shrugged and glanced at Devon. "You find the water?"

She nodded, and only now did she remember the wondrous city that she hadn't yet told them about.

"Morgan's still in there, exploring," she said. "We were

just about to go to the water when the alarm sounded. It's a running stream, and plenty of it."

Alonzo grinned at Danziger and slapped dust from his clothing. "Bath time."

"There's more," Devon continued excitedly. "There's a city in there."

Both men looked at her in startlement, and the others crowded around to listen.

"What do you mean, a city?"

She laughed, pleased by their surprise. "There's an enormous cavern, big as a space dock, and inside it is a complete city, smallish, of course, but it has towers and buildings of all descriptions. Everything's made out of white stone like these columns, and it's so beautiful you won't believe your eyes."

"A sacred city," Alonzo said thoughtfully.

"Morgan's convinced he's going to find temples and treasure," Devon said in amusement, "but as far as I'm concerned just the sights are reward enough. You all have to come inside and see it."

Danziger frowned. "I have repairs to get back to."

"There's no hurry, is there?" True said. She came up to Devon. "You said I could go inside after you checked it out."

Devon glanced at Danziger, who shrugged. "Sure," he told his daughter. "Go on, and take that dratted koba with you. I don't need its help."

True grinned. "I'll be back soon to help. Promise."

"Come on!" Julia called out. "Everybody, come and see."

Bess, the children, and Yale clustered around her, and she led them inside, pointing out features like a tour guide.

Zero started to follow them.

"Not you!" Danziger snapped. "Get back over here and work."

Zero wheeled around obediently. "I am always willing to work. That's what I'm programmed for."

Danziger went back to the TransRover, Zero lumbering behind him like a huge dog, and began pulling out tools.

Devon glanced at Alonzo. "You have the most amazing luck. Ready to see what we've found?"

He shook his head. "Not really." He hesitated, his gaze straying to the dead bull. "I promised the Terrian we wouldn't kill another buffalo."

"It was you or it, Solace," Danziger said, lifting out an electronic wrench set.

"Yes, I know, but I promised."

"If there's trouble," Devon said, "we'll have to deal with it later. Go in there and see what we've found."

The pilot met her gaze, then shrugged and walked toward the gateway.

"We're waiting, Alonzo!" Julia called. "Come on."

He quickened his step, pausing only to glance back at the dead buffalo one last time before he vanished into the darkness.

Nightfall saw them settled in a camp just outside the city's walls. With the lamps shining around them, the cavern didn't seem quite as huge or daunting. Danziger had finished overhauling the fluid lines on the TransRover and had repaired the cracked solar panel on the DuneRail. The water tanks were a job still to be tackled. He was sitting now with Alonzo and Morgan, sketching a diagram of how he wanted to remove the tanks from the TransRover altogether and bring them down to the ground for repair.

"With the ground supporting their weight, I can get a better seam closure than if I'm trying to weld with them suspended. I'll rig up a winch system tomorrow on Zero, but I'll need you two to steady the lines."

Carrying a towel, Devon walked past them, aware that Morgan was barely listening. His eyes strayed back to the city rising above them; avid impatience chased across his features.

She caught up with Bess, who was also going to bathe in the stream. At some point it passed beneath the city's walls, then emerged on the eastern side, but they were going to bathe upstream, where they had found a natural pool formed in the rock, with a short waterfall spilling below.

Julia was already there ahead of them with True, whose young body looked slender and tanned in the glow of lamplight. She poised on a rock and dived in, then bobbed to the surface and paddled vigorously.

"She shouldn't be diving," Bess said in concern. "We don't know how deep that pool is."

"About four meters," Devon replied, pulling her towel off her shoulder. "True checked it with a scanner."

"Efficient, as usual," Bess said, smiling.

"She comes by it naturally."

"She's a fortunate child to have such a good father," Bess said.

Devon nodded. She and Bess had spent hours skinning the buffalo and preserving the meat for later use. Their supply of preservative was running low; when it finally ran out, they would have to sun-dry meat into jerky. Self-reliance, Devon thought, feeling tired but happy. She and Bess were filthy with blood, dirt, and hair, but the job had been completed. A supper of grilled buffalo steaks had been incredibly delicious, the meat quite dark but tender. Devon was determined to save the hide for leather goods they would need later, and she was already turning over ideas in her mind for a way to capture some of the calves. If they could domesticate these creatures, she thought they would be extremely useful in numerous ways. It had to be attempted.

But right now all she wanted was to be clean again.

She undressed quickly and slid into the water, gasping at how icy cold it was. The shock nearly robbed her of breath, and at first all she could do was tread water furiously and shiver.

When she emerged a short time later, shaking with cold but feeling invigorated, she toweled off briskly and dressed in clean clothing.

Bess was already washing clothes, seemingly tireless. Devon was amazed by her stamina.

"It's wonderful to wash off that gritty dust, isn't it?" Bess said happily.

"Like heaven," Devon said.

Julia murmured agreement.

True climbed up on the rock and dived in again. Her skin was goose pimpled with cold, but she seemed impervious to it. With a whoop she surfaced and splashed about.

"We may have to put a rope on her to get her out," Julia said.

The three women smiled at each other.

"Yes," Bess said. "The men will be wanting to come up for their baths soon. We can't keep them waiting forever."

But when they returned to the camp, only Alonzo, Yale, and Danziger sat there.

Bess looked around in puzzlement, laying down her bundle of washed clothing and slinging her braided hair back over her shoulder. "Where's Morgan?"

Danziger was reading a manual and didn't respond, but Yale looked up.

"He said he wanted to go for a walk."

"How odd," Bess said.

Devon frowned at the buildings rising above them. "He's

gone exploring again," she said, displeased. "Bess, you need to talk to him. Convince him there's no treasure. Even if he found any, it doesn't belong to us. This is an ancient Terrian place, something special. We mustn't disturb any part of it."

Bess nodded. "I agree. But you know how he is when he takes a notion in his head. He doesn't give up."

"Well, talk to him anyway," Devon said, sharply enough to make Bess frown. "We've offended the Terrians enough as it is. And besides, it isn't necessarily safe for him to wander off by himself."

"I'll tell him," Bess said. "But he's not very good at following orders. Especially mine."

She smiled as she said it, but there was something wistful in her expression that tugged at Devon.

"That man doesn't appreciate you the way he should," Julia announced, spreading her clothing near the fire, which crackled briskly, exuding heat that was welcome after their swim. The temperature inside the cave seemed to remain constant, but it was chilly.

"Of course he does," Bess said instantly. She was always ready to defend Morgan.

Devon didn't argue with her. She'd said enough already, but as she sent Uly off for his bath and got his bunk unfolded and prepared, she couldn't help but glance frequently toward the silent, abandoned city beside them. She saw no glimmers of torchlight, heard no sound from within its confines. Morgan had no business wandering alone in there. They had already agreed to go exploring tomorrow. He could have waited, the greedy idiot.

Uly and Yale came back, and Devon warmed her shivering son with a hot drink and a brisk towel rub before tucking him into bed. By lamplight, she brushed Uly's hair back from his face while he yawned sleepily.

"This was a neat day," he said. "I like exploring in caves. Tomorrow True and I are going to look around the city."

"You need to get some sleep."

"Boy, wasn't that buffalo something?" he said, his eyes still glowing with the memory of Alonzo's narrow escape. "Are we going to catch any of them?"

"I hope to. Later on, if we can."

"I want the first calf we catch," he said. "I can tame it. I know I can. True's not the only one who's good with animals."

Devon didn't tell her son that he lacked True's patience or sense of responsibility. "You better get some sleep."

His blue eyes drooped closed then struggled open. "Mom?"

"Yes?"

"You, uh, it's kind of nice when you sing. If you want to."

Her smile broadened. These days Uly was too much the boy, too independent, to want much obvious affection from her or to come out and ask her for a lullaby, but he still wasn't quite as independent as he pretended. Still stroking his hair, she began to hum softly. In a few minutes his eyes drifted closed.

She turned down the lamp and left him to get her own bunk ready.

By then Morgan came staggering back to camp.

He was white-faced with fatigue and grumbled a reply to Bess's soft-voiced question. He shook his head and stalked off to bathe.

In a few minutes he returned, his wet hair dripping around his face and his dirty clothes bundled unwashed beneath his arm. He tossed them down for Bess to gather and saw Devon frowning at him.

He scowled back but joined her. "Bess says you don't want me exploring."

His tone made it a challenge.

"You can explore all you want," Devon said evenly, not wanting to pick a quarrel, "but you shouldn't go alone, for obvious safety reasons."

He snorted and combed his hair back into its usual ponytail. "The cavern's been scanned. There's nothing down here to worry about."

"Some dangers don't show up on the scanners," she said, feeling as though she were lecturing to Uly—and getting about as much attention. "Bottomless pools, sinkholes, rockfalls. That sort of thing."

"No," he said smugly. "You don't want me finding treasure before the rest of you."

"There's no treasure down here," she said sharply.

His eyebrows shot up. "Oh, yeah? I found the temple."

She blinked despite her annoyance. "How do you know?"

"It's pretty obvious. More sun disks and moon carvings, a big altar out on the portico. That sort of thing."

"You haven't disturbed anything, have you?"

"So what?" he said dismissively. "It's all old—"

"The Terrians don't want us here."

"So they can run us out," he said with a shrug.

"They might just do that."

"We've got Zero posted outside with Walman and Baines to back him up. The Terrians can't get in here without someone sounding an alarm."

"Morgan, that's not true—"

"Relax. I haven't done anything to the temple. I couldn't get in. But I will. Don't worry about that."

"I *do* worry. We're trying to get on good terms with the Terrians—"

"So this one tribe out here in the desert gets mad," he said. "So what? That doesn't mean we can't be on good terms with some of the other tribes. They won't know. They probably won't care."

"You can't make an assumption like that."

"You worry too much," he said with a smile, and walked away from her before she could argue further.

Devon gritted her teeth, exasperated with his stubbornness. Someone had to worry, she told herself. Someone had to exercise a little responsibility around here. Morgan was suffering from a bad case of gold fever. She just hoped it didn't get all of them into trouble.

Chapter 7

• • • • • • • ⬤

Danziger emerged from the cave and walked out beneath the overhang. Sunlight made him squint. The air was warm already, like an oven despite the shade. He walked toward the TransRover, intending to continue his repairs, but out of nowhere five Terrians suddenly appeared and surrounded him.

Silent and tall, they glared at him and closed in.

"Baines!" he called in alarm, seeking help. "Walman!"

But the area was deserted save for him and the Terrians. Their long-fingered hands gripped him with a strength he could not shake off. He found himself dragged down the ramp and pushed to the ground.

Out here the sun blazed mercilessly, light glaring off the cliffs and hot ground. There was no wind, no sound of anything except his own rapid heartbeat. He tried to scramble to his feet, but they pushed him down again and stood in a ring around him, tall and inscrutable, their faces in shadow against the sun overhead.

"Let me go!" he said. "I've done nothing against you. Let me go."

"Firestriker."

None of the Terrians spoke, yet the word entered his mind. Danziger frowned in puzzlement. He wasn't someone the Terrians communicated with. So why had they sought him out now?

He knew, even as the thought entered his mind. They had as yet made no accusation, yet the name they'd assigned to him was enough. A sense of guilt rose inside him. "I shot the buffalo in defense," he said. "It attacked us. It would have hurt Alonzo, possibly the children. I had to—"

One of the Terrians poured hot sand over him. Another followed suit, and another, the warm grains trickling over his skin and clothing. He held up his hand to stop them, and suddenly he was half-buried in the sand, and it was rising steadily around him. It was warm and very heavy, pinning his limbs. He could not brush it off, could not move his arms.

Panic gripped him hard. He couldn't be buried alive. They couldn't—

Gasping, Danziger sat bolt upright on his bunk and stared at the darkness surrounding him. The camp fires had burned low; only a few embers still glowed among the ashes. Around him came the steady breathing of his companions.

He gulped in air and rubbed the sweat from his face, trying to calm down. It had been a dream, just a dream.

Or had the Terrians been trying to tell him something?

Half-angrily he dismissed the thought. Alonzo was the contact they'd chosen to communicate with, not him. It was probably just ill-digested buffalo meat giving him nightmares.

He caught himself smoothing his blanket over and over with an unsteady hand, unconsciously reassuring himself that there was no sand to smother him. When he realized what he was doing, he stopped and clenched the blanket in his fist.

Just a dream, he told himself again.

He forced himself to lie down, but it was a long time before he went back to sleep.

A deep, steady sound awakened Devon. Puzzled by it, at first she thought a buffalo had somehow found its way inside the caverns, then her mind shook off sleep and identified the sound as steady drumming. She sat up and stared across the sleeping camp at the ghostly white city standing silent within the cave's shadows.

Where was the drumming coming from? What did it mean?

Throwing off her blanket, she started to call out and rouse the others, but the sound died in her throat.

A Terrian stood beside her bunk, holding his lightning stick. She gulped a little and stared without moving, not certain what to do.

The drumming grew louder. She looked around, but she could not find the source for it.

The Terrian stepped closer until he loomed over her. She knew there was no point in speaking to him. That wasn't the way Terrians communicated.

He lifted a small, carved bowl over her. Her gaze followed it, staring as he tipped it and poured out the contents.

Cold water hit her forehead with a splash that made her blink. Startled, she lifted her hand to wipe the wetness away—and came awake from a dream that had been too vivid to be anything but real.

Yet here she was lying in her bunk, wiping her face again and again. Her skin was dry. No water had been spilled on her.

Frowning and shivering, she listened in the quiet, but there was no sound. Certainly no one was beating a drum.

She brushed back her hair from her face and blew out her breath, feeling strange and unsettled. Had it been a normal dream, or had the Terrian been trying to tell her something? If the latter, what?

Sighing, she found herself too wide awake to go back to sleep. Leaving her bunk, she put on her boots and took a torch, which she shielded with her hand until she was away from the camp.

Carefully she picked her way back to the stream, climbing up the rocks past the waterfall to the pool. She settled beside the pool, with her back against cold stone, and gazed out over the city.

A tiny rustle of sound startled her.

She jumped up, tense and wide-eyed, and shone her torch around. A pair of eyes glowed at her, and she froze a second before the koba crept forward into the light. It stared up at her, its pointed ears swiveling.

"What are you doing up?" she asked, gasping in relief. She sank back down.

The koba crouched, imitating her actions.

Smiling, she reached out to pet it, and it patted her back, making a contented sound deep in its throat.

"Devon?" whispered True.

Startled again, Devon looked up and saw True peering around a rock at her. Devon frowned in concern. "Hey, what are you doing up here?"

True shrugged, evading her gaze. "Just hanging out."

"Something wrong?" Devon persisted. "Can't sleep?"

True shrugged again and joined her.

Devon wanted to question her, but held back.

True looked restless and uneasy. Brushing her hair back from her face, she slapped her hands idly on her knees.

"I'm not sleepy," she said.

"How come?"

True cast her a sharp look, which the koba imitated. "How come you're up?"

Devon started to flip out an evasive answer, but she knew the only way to deal with True was to be straight with her. "I had a dream."

True blinked. "A Terrian kind of dream? Like Alonzo gets?"

"I think so, but I'm not sure. It was strange. I keep thinking I ought to understand it, but maybe it was just a dream." She sighed. "I don't know. Did you have a dream about the Terrians?"

"No," True said in a small voice.

"What then?"

"Aw, I don't know. I can't really remember it. I just felt kind of strange when I woke up. Sad or something." She looked out across the cavern toward the city. "I wonder why they left the city."

"Well—"

"No, I mean, *why*. It's so pretty. Nothing like the way they live now. Why would they change that?"

"People do change," Devon said. "Sometimes whether they want to or not. Sometimes disease wipes out a community. Skills and knowledge get lost. Sometimes people get to wanting something different than what they've always known. They leave home and strike out. That's what we did."

"You did," True said quickly. "Dad and I aren't going to stay here forever."

Devon felt a little sad at the girl's words, but she nodded, accepting it. "I know. You miss the station, don't you?"

"Yeah. I mean, this is okay, now that I've gotten used to it. But the station has so much to do. Things are happening all the time. Ships come in, and there's the maintenance. It's exciting." She sighed. "Sometimes when we're just going along all day, looking at scenery, I want to scream because it's so boring. Then a day like this happens, and I'm glad I came here."

"Well, I'm glad you're here," Devon said, smiling at her. "And I'm glad you and Uly have learned to get along."

True grinned sheepishly. "Yeah."

Then her gaze wandered back to the city. "It's still sad, though. They shouldn't have left it. They shouldn't have forgotten it."

"I don't think they did forget it," Devon said slowly, frowning as she tried to sort out what she meant. "They still know it's here. They guard it."

"But they won't live in it. I wish I knew why."

"Maybe someday we'll know the answer, but I have a feeling there's a lot on this planet we'll never understand."

True yawned, and Devon handed the sleeping koba to her. "Maybe you two better get back to bed."

"Maybe it's morning," True argued sleepily, snuggling the koba in her arms. "You can't tell, down here in the dark."

"You've got about four hours of sleep left before it'll be time to get up."

Devon got to her feet and beckoned to True. Reluctantly the girl climbed down the rocks after her.

"Let's go explore it now," True said suddenly as they reached the foot of the waterfall. Her eyes glistened in the torchlight. "Forget about waiting until morning. What difference does it make? I want to see what it's like."

Devon frowned, a little surprised by her eagerness. She looked almost like Morgan when he'd talked about finding treasure.

"There's plenty of time," she said. "Besides, you want to wait for Uly, don't you?"

True looked up at her with admiration. "I'd rather go with you."

"Well, I don't have time to explore, I'm afraid," Devon said. "I have a lot of work to do tomorrow."

"Please?" True urged, taking Devon's hand. Her own was icy cold. "Please come with me?"

For a moment there was something odd about her expression, something too intense. Devon drew away instinctively, and her sharp movement made True blink and rub her eyes.

"If you won't, then I guess you won't," True said with sudden indifference. She stepped past Devon and headed back to camp. "Night."

Devon stared after her a few moments before following much more slowly. She watched True get back in her bunk and settle under her blanket. It seemed that the moment True's head touched the pillow she was asleep, but Devon went on watching her for a long time.

How odd. True wasn't one to tag along after her. The girl was usually busy working with her father or else off exploring on her own. She was feisty and independent, and she usually held adults at a distance, as though sensing that her childhood would be coming to an end in the next year or so. But who knew with kids on the brink of adolescence? Maybe it was normal for the girl to be up in the middle of the night, staring at the ghost city. Maybe it was normal for her to urge Devon to go with her right then.

But Devon couldn't convince herself that it was.

She remembered the strange expression in True's eyes, how for a moment it hadn't seemed to be True urging her at all.

Devon gave herself a shake and got back in her bunk. She was crazy to be thinking such things. Maybe she was letting the atmosphere of this place get to her. Soon, if she didn't watch it, her imagination would be running as wild as Uly's.

But just the same she couldn't stop herself from looking out at the city standing so silent and still. Maybe ghosts still walked its dead streets. Maybe she should have heeded the Terrian warnings after all.

She shivered and pulled the blanket up to her ears. Maybe she should stop thinking such things and go back to sleep.

Chapter 8

In the morning, True sought out Bess, who was checking bedding and clothes for mending to be done. "Hi, Bess."

Bess always had a warm smile for her. She seemed to be a friendly person, but she liked doing domestic things that didn't interest True at all. True usually steered clear of her projects.

"Hi, True," Bess said. "Did you sleep well?"

True frowned a moment, then shrugged. "Uh, I guess so. Why?"

"Oh, several people seemed to have had a lot of dreams last night. Morgan tossed and turned for hours, muttering in his sleep. And Devon said she had a nightmare too. I slept fine, though, and so did Alonzo."

True was impatient to get on with her day. "Yeah, great," she said, feeling that the conversation was stupid. "Look,

Bess, would you keep the koba for me? I'm going exploring and I don't need it getting in the way."

Bess looked surprised. Usually True took the little animal with her everywhere. "Sure, I'll be glad to, as long as it doesn't try to eat my thread."

True grinned. "It understands the word 'no.' But don't slap at it or he'll slap back."

She pushed the koba off her shoulder and handed it over to Bess, who scratched its chin and cooed to it. The koba's beady eyes brightened, and it cooed back, reaching for Bess's chin. Leaving Bess laughing, True hurried off to collect Uly.

He was slow getting started this morning. She'd been by twice already and he still hadn't been ready. She told herself that if he wasn't ready this time, she would go without him. As for herself, she was prepared with her canteen and a supply of quick-energy bars. She also had her own private tool kit in her pack. It was made up of an odd assortment of things; some of the tools she'd made herself, others she'd appropriated from her father's collection, old things he didn't really want anymore, and still others she'd acquired from hanging around the repair docks at the station—worn-out stuff, thrown away or discarded. But it was useful to her to have a couple of laser probes, picks, a solar drill, which probably wouldn't work down here, and a measure. She'd also tossed in a scanner and a spare torch.

The pack settled easily on her straight shoulders, and her heart was thumping with excitement. She'd seen Morgan set out early for his own explorations after borrowing some tools from her dad. True grinned to herself. She figured she and Uly could find more neat stuff than he could.

But not if Uly didn't come on.

"Uly!" she called, waving at him. "Aren't you ready yet?"

He was still munching on his breakfast of dried fruit and

some of Bess's bread. He had his pack slung over his shoulders, but no canteen, and one of his boots wasn't on yet. Yale was lecturing him in a soft, stern voice. Uly nodded now and then to show he was listening, but his gaze cut around to meet True's and he rolled his eyes.

She had to clamp her mouth tight to hold back a giggle. "Come on," she said to him, interrupting the tutor. "You're wasting time. Let's go."

"Okay."

Uly stuffed the remainder of his breakfast into his mouth, making his cheeks bulge, and swiftly bent down to put on his second boot. True fidgeted around. Her dad had already gone outside to work. She was afraid if they didn't get started, he would call her to come help him.

"Check your headset to make sure it's working," Yale said.

Uly thumped it. "Yeah."

"And you have a new charge on your torch?"

"If you put it in for me, I do." Uly grinned at the old man as he said it.

True sighed to herself. Uly really was too spoiled for words. But finally he was ready, and they went racing across the cavern toward the city, where the beam of light from the fissure overhead shone down like a spotlight to illuminate it.

But there remained more shadows than light, and as they neared the walls, True slowed down. She switched on her torch and began to watch her footing. Uly raced on heedlessly until loose gravel underfoot made him slip and nearly fall.

He paused, panting hard, and glanced back at her with a grin. Beyond him stood the city gates, long since rotted to dust, leaving a broad gap in the wall. The air smelled of damp stone and blew cool against their hot faces.

"Switch on your torch," True said.

"I can see—"

"Switch it on. There's not going to be much light when we get in among the buildings. You know how pitch-black caves can be. Like space."

Fiercely she watched until he did as she said. Then she preceded him through the gate.

They found a maze of narrow streets awaiting them. True pulled the scanner out of her pack with a secret feeling of having dared the forbidden, and activated it.

"Hey!" Uly said. "How'd you get that? We're not supposed to be using the equipment."

"No one needs it right now," True said coolly, aware of Uly's mouth gaping open in awe while she pretended to keep her attention locked on the scanner. She entered the proper settings and watched on the tiny screen as it created a map grid of the city.

Uly pressed against her shoulder, watching. "Wow," he said. "How'd you learn to make it do that?"

"I know how to do a lot of things," True said. "Look, there's Morgan over on the east side. Let's keep away from him."

"Yeah. We don't need him in our way."

True took a directional bearing and entered it into the scanner so they could find their way back if they got lost, then she chose one of the streets at random and headed down it. Uly crowded on her heels, swinging his torch around wildly to illuminate empty windows, gaping doorways, and carved cornerstones.

"Agh!" Uly shouted, bumping into True so hard he almost knocked her down.

She whirled around, her heart thumping, and gripped him. Suddenly their torchlight was bouncing everywhere and she couldn't see anything. "What is it? What is it?" she demanded.

Uly's blue eyes were so wide she could see white all the way around his irises. His face was pale, and he kept staring up into the gloom although he wouldn't shine his torch in that direction. "A f-face," he stammered. "Looking right at me."

"Where?" True whispered.

He kept crowding back against her as though to push her on, but she planted her feet and wouldn't budge. His fear was infectious, and she was tempted to flee, but then whatever it was would probably chase them. Swallowing hard, she aimed her torch upward and shone it over the wall of the building that loomed above them.

A face leered at her from the darkness, stark white and twisted in a grimace that made her gasp. She dropped her torch, and it went rolling into the darkness on the ground.

Meanwhile, Uly was shoving her with both hands now. "See?" he gasped. "*See?* I told you to run!"

"No, wait," she said, pushing him back.

"But, True—"

"No! Just calm down," she said sharply. She'd regained her wits and was already ashamed of her own reaction. She bent down and retrieved her torch then shone it upward at the face again. "It's a carving, silly. Just a piece of stone. See?"

Uly's harsh breathing slowed. He gulped audibly and tried to recover his cool. "Okay," he said. "I knew that. I was just trying to see if I could rattle you. Guess you passed the test."

She rolled her eyes at him, exasperated by his sudden bravado. He met her scornful gaze and looked down. A dull red stained his cheeks.

"Yeah," she said, hitching her pack higher on her shoulders. "Let's go. And stop being so jumpy. The place is totally deserted, except for Morgan."

"Okay," Uly said. He shifted his torch from hand to hand. "Sure. Okay. Let's go."

"Right."

Again she led the way, picking up the pace this time. Soon they turned a corner, crossed an arching bridge, and found themselves in a kind of small square. The buildings were all fairly low, no more than two or three stories, and narrow. Some of them had crumbled. Piles of rubble lay here and there. Most were missing their roofs as though they had fallen in.

Uly climbed on top of a heap of stones and brick and swung his torch around. "Let's go in the biggest building over there."

"Okay."

True set out for it, passing a fountain now dry and dusty. She paused beside it, aware of the stream rushing somewhere beneath her feet. She could hear the running water, could feel its damp coldness rising up through the stone. For a moment she put her hand on the rim of the fountain and slid her palm back and forth across the gritty surface. It was in no shape she recognized, and the carvings were very strange. They hurt her eyes if she stared too long at them. Blinking, she pushed herself on after Uly, who hadn't waited for her.

"I wonder why the fountain doesn't work anymore," she said.

"It's probably broken." Uly paused in a doorway and peered inside cautiously. "Do you think any of this will fall on us?"

"Not if we're careful. Watch where you go, and don't break a leg or something."

"Relax," he said with scorn. "I'm not a baby."

As though to prove it, he went inside the building first. True hesitated, studying its features and trying to figure out what it had once been used for. A porch with narrow columns that looked upside down had once stood over the entrance, but all that had fallen, and a wide crack bisected the floor.

She climbed inside and shone her torch around. Uly was nowhere in sight. For a second she felt alarm. "Uly? Where'd you go?"

"Come on!" he called, his voice distant.

She frowned. "Don't get so far ahead!" she called. "Remember, some of this could fall on you."

"Aw, come on! Don't worry so much. You're starting to sound like my mom."

True's gaze narrowed. If he didn't stop insulting her by comparing her to grown-ups, she was going to leave him to find his own way home. "Yeah? Well, remember I've got the scanner."

He didn't answer, and she picked her way hurriedly over shifting piles of rubble, stirring up ancient dust that made her sneeze. When she finally caught up with him, he was outside, sitting on a big square stone beyond where the wall had fallen down completely.

"You know, I bet most of this place is a wreck," he said.

She looked around. "I think you're right."

He tossed down the fragment of carved stone he'd been examining and dusted off his pants. "Let's keep looking. Maybe it'll get better."

The next time they entered one of the buildings, they chose one that looked intact. But inside they found that some of the upper floors had fallen in, and this one had a sour, musty smell that True didn't like.

They backed out hastily.

"Whew," Uly said, scrubbing his nose with the back of his hand. "What lives in there?"

"Something we don't want to meet."

After a while the streets grew wider and the buildings more ornate. They seemed to have lasted through time better too. Fewer showed signs of wear and damage, and when True and Uly came to another square, it was far more spacious and closer to where the beam of sunlight shone down. They almost didn't need their torches. True climbed up on the side of the fountain and stood on her tiptoes to gaze into its middle tier. "I wish we could make these work again."

"Forget it," Uly said impatiently. "They're all broken."

"Why should they be? I don't see any signs of damage."

"Too old," Uly said.

But True wasn't willing to settle for his easy explanation. She patted along the stone sides of the fountain. This one wasn't rough like the first. Its sides had been polished smooth long ago. When she brushed the dust away, it felt almost silky beneath her fingertips.

"You *can* work, can't you?" she murmured to it as though it were alive. "Hey! Remember what your mom said about this whole place?"

"Nope," Uly said. He was picking up more of the carved fragments and putting them in his pack.

"Everything's an illusion."

"That was just to hide the way in."

"Maybe it hides the way this fountain works. It looks dry, but it probably still operates."

"No, it doesn't."

True kept running her hands over the surface of the basins, trying to find some secret knob or lever. She leaned too far, trying to reach around the back side, and nearly lost her balance. Only a quick grab of the stone saved her. But the middle basin she was holding onto shifted clockwise in response to her weight.

She heard a gurgle of water. Astonished, she looked down and saw the shine of it in her torchlight.

"I did it!" she yelled.

Uly tossed down a piece of carving. "No way."

She gripped the basin with both hands and twisted it farther. The gurgle became a sputtering stream that bubbled up, splashing her boots. She jumped off quickly, and the water jetted on up to the top, still sputtering now and then, as though trying to work out air bubbles in the passageway. Then it began to flow down, filling the basins one by one, and spilling over.

True stared at it, fascinated by how it worked. "It's beautiful," she breathed. She dipped her hand into the water. It was so cold it seemed to burn her fingers.

"It's just an old fountain," Uly said.

She flipped water at him, and he ducked. "There aren't any fountains like this on the station. I've only seen them in holos before."

"Are you going to leave it on?" Uly asked.

"Why not?"

She was proud of having brought forth some life in the old city. The sound of the gently splashing water was reassuring after so much heavy silence. "That looks like a house," she said, pointing. "Let's try it."

They wandered through room after room, stared at mysterious wall ledges and intricate depressions and ridges carved into the floors. Uly even ventured up the stone steps running along one wall, but he came down quickly.

"Nothing," he said in disgust. "Just an empty room with a window that overlooks the fountain.

True gazed around and finally figured out what had been puzzling her all along. "You know," she said slowly, "this place is weird."

"No kidding."

"No, I mean, there's nothing here but the buildings."

"So?"

"So look around. People lived here, right?"

Uly shrugged. "I guess so. Maybe it was a bank or something."

"Well, even so there should be some gear and furniture and stuff. That's what we came to look for, isn't it?"

"Yeah." Uly looked around with more interest, a crease between his brows. "You're right. Everything's empty."

"Not a glass or a bowl," True said.

"Not even tables and chairs."

They looked at each other.

"Your mom said maybe they just got tired of living here and moved away. Maybe they took everything with them," True said.

"I think it was a plague, something really gross that eats your flesh so that you turn black and spotted with pus and die in a matter of hours." Uly gripped his throat and made horrible, strangling noises.

"Don't be silly," she said impatiently. "If that had happened, all their stuff would still be here. We'd find their skeletons."

"You're right." He sighed. "This place is kind of boring."

"Yeah." She felt disappointed after all her anticipation.

"Well, come on upstairs and look at your fountain. It's kind of neat from that angle."

"It is?" she said, brightening.

"Yeah." He grinned at her and raced up the steps.

True walked up them more cautiously, keeping herself pressed closely against the wall in case her weight proved too much. She was aware that she was taking a physical risk her father wouldn't approve of, but she did it anyway because Uly had already shown her it could be done.

The steps seemed sound enough, and by the time she

reached the top she relaxed and stopped worrying about the staircase falling with her.

There was only a spacious single room on this story, marked by three windows facing in different directions. Uly was already standing by one. She glanced out and saw her fountain bubbling away.

From up here, however, she gained a new perspective on the city. The maze of streets seemed less confusing. She could see that the better buildings formed a sort of ring around the center.

As soon as she figured that out, she moved to another window, one much smaller, and leaned out.

She could see the beam of sunlight shining more strongly now, becoming wider and brighter as the sun rose into the sky. She figured whoever had built the city had planned it around the way the sunlight moved through that hole up there in the top of the cavern. They seemed like the kind of people who would take notice of details like that. Little motes of dust danced in the light, swirling almost in patterns.

True caught herself staring, almost mesmerized, and drew back with a blink.

Uly was at her shoulder, tapping it. "True? Hey, True, wake up! Are you coming, or not? We can't stay up here forever."

"Why not?" she asked dreamily, then frowned at herself. What was wrong with her? She rubbed her face, feeling as though she'd lost some time. But she wasn't going to ask Uly about it. She was older. What did he know, anyway?

He snapped his fingers in front of her face. "Hello. Anybody home?"

She scowled and shoved his hand away. "Quit."

"Then stop staring into space like you've had your mind wiped," he retorted. "Let's go."

"Just a minute. I want to look out through these other windows."

"There's just one more—"

But she hurried across the room to it without listening. It was a strange rhomboid shape, like no window she'd ever seen, but from this vantage point she had a better view of the beam of sunlight and what section of the city it was shining on.

She glimpsed the curve of a tall wall, and leaned out in an effort to see better.

Uly grabbed the back of her shirt, making her jump. She nearly pitched out headlong, and only his grip helped her pull back.

Breathless and scared, she turned on him angrily. "What's the idea, pushing me like that?"

"I didn't push you," he said, wide-eyed. "I was afraid you were going to fall."

"I nearly did, thanks to you."

Uly began to look angry too. "I didn't push you. You were leaning out too far. If it hadn't been for me, you'd have broken your neck."

"Okay, forget it," she said, refusing to continue the argument.

"You were leaning out," he insisted stubbornly. "Admit it."

"Okay!" She hooked her hair behind her ears with exasperation. "Okay. I saw something. I guess I wasn't paying attention."

"Let's go down before you jump out or something," Uly said, eyeing her as though she'd suddenly grown two heads. "You're really getting strange."

She didn't answer, feeling her mind starting to drift again. Dreamily she wandered after him, following him down the steps and outside.

There, as though the fresher air of the cavern cleared something away, she blinked and felt much better, focused again, herself again. She rubbed her face and frowned.

"What was that in there?"

"I don't know, but you started looking kind of geared out," Uly said in concern. "And you got mad at me for no reason."

"I did?" She couldn't remember.

"Did you eat breakfast this morning?"

His question irritated her. "Of course," she snapped.

"Well, maybe you'd better eat something else. I've got some energy bars in my pack."

"I'm not hungry." But she was suddenly, ravenously so.

They sat down by the fountain and wolfed two bars each, then drank the icy water. It was so cold it made her teeth hurt, but she felt fresh and exhilarated again.

"I think we'd better stay out of the houses," she said. "It was too weird in there."

"Sounds good to me," Uly agreed. "Unless they have some stuff in them, it's a waste of time to go in anyway."

True scrambled to her feet and took a new bearing. What she'd seen from the window didn't show on the scanner. Puzzled, she ran a check, but the scanner seemed to be working properly.

"Problem?"

"No," she said too quickly. She scanned again, but the wall didn't show on the scanner. "How odd."

"What?" Uly said, a hint of worry creeping into his voice. "You've lost the bearing. We can't get back."

"No, silly. I saw another wall up there from the window."

"What kind of wall?"

"You know. Like around something. It's right in the center of the city, over there where the towers are. Where the light's shining."

"Oh." Uly looked in that direction. "I don't see any wall."

"Of course not. You're not tall enough to see over the buildings. But up there, I saw it. I want to go to it."

Without waiting for his reply, she set off at a fast trot, sometimes almost running. The streets abruptly stopped going in the direction she wanted and veered away at right angles. True stopped and turned around in frustration, then remembered that everything was an illusion.

She frowned at the building that stood directly across their path and started walking toward it quickly.

"True?" Uly said, hurrying beside her. "Hey, True? We said we weren't going in any more buildings. Remember?"

"I don't think this is a building," she said grimly.

"Of course it is. It's right in front of us."

"You didn't think the fountain would work, but it did."

He shut up and followed her without further protest.

When they came up to the building, she saw that it wasn't an actual structure at all, but only a false facade. "See?" she said triumphantly and gripped his hand. "Come on, let's go through."

She pulled him through the doorway and had time only to register that suddenly it was pitch dark, as though her torch had gone out. Suddenly there was no solid ground under their feet.

With a yelp, she was falling, tumbling head over heels down a steep incline. She dropped her torch in the process, and the darkness became even blacker.

Screaming, she fell deep into it.

Chapter 9

Danziger's furious bellow almost rivaled that of the buffalo.

It came in over Devon's gear with a volume that jerked her to her feet. Wincing, she adjusted volume level, but it didn't help much. Danziger was fuming and swearing as though he didn't realize he was broadcasting.

"John," Devon tried to break in. "Hey, calm down before you fry the circuits. What's wrong?"

He was still swearing and didn't answer her. Devon blinked at some of the things she heard and swiftly turned off her gear. Glancing around, she saw Bess doing the same thing with wide eyes. Julia looked at them and shook her head. Yale rose stiffly to his feet and frowned.

Seconds later Danziger appeared on the ledge above them and came hurtling down without heed for how narrow or steep it was. Every other stride seemed to knock pebbles over the edge, and they went clattering to the ground below.

By the time he reached the camp, he was out of breath and red-faced.

"What's wrong?" Devon demanded, but he brushed past her and went straight to Bess.

"Where is he?" he demanded.

She stared at Danziger as though he'd lost his mind, but after a short hesitation, she said, "Morgan?"

"Damn right, Morgan."

Bess flinched at his tone, and Julia intervened. "Calm down, Danziger," she said sharply. "Yelling at us isn't helping the situation, whatever it is."

He listened to her and drew in a couple of breaths before he said anything else. And although his tone grew milder, his eyes still blazed furiously and he tended to bite off each word. "Your husband," he said, glaring at Bess again, "has taken Zero to God knows where. He doesn't answer his gear channel."

She blinked and instantly adjusted her gear as though she were checking. "Morgan?" she said. "Morgan, come in."

She waited but got no response. Something flickered in her pretty brown eyes. "He's fine," she said defensively. "He often shuts off his channel when he wants to think over something. It's a way of insuring his privacy."

"Not when he's stolen the robot," Danziger said grimly.

Devon had to protest that. "He hasn't stolen Zero. Borrowed him—"

"Yeah, fine. Call it what you want. I need Zero to lift off the tanks. Morgan knew that. Why the hell—"

"Swearing at us isn't going to help matters," Devon told him. She knew now why Morgan had looked so smug last night. "He's taken Zero to smash in the door of a temple he's found. That won't take long."

Danziger lifted his hands and let them fall in mute

exasperation. "Treasure hunting," he said in scorn. "Meanwhile, Alonzo and I are sitting on our thumbs, unable to get any work done."

"It's a desecration," Yale said sternly, "to destroy ancient artifacts. Not to mention the—"

"Yeah," Danziger said impatiently. "We've got Terrians mad because we're here in the first place, now he's using Zero to knock down a few walls, and I can't get any work done. That means we can't leave as soon as we meant to, which means the Terrians will be even madder."

Danziger paused for breath and ran a hand over his chin. Devon blinked at him, not sure when she'd seen him lose his temper like this. On one of the bunks, the koba jumped up and down, ran its paw along its chin, and chattered angrily.

Julia smiled, then hastily wiped the expression off her face.

Danziger, however, was busy glaring at Bess again.

"I'm sorry," she apologized softly. "I had no idea he meant to—"

"Skip it," Danziger said with sudden gruffness. His frown deepened. "I didn't mean to come down here and yell at you. I know it's not your fault. I just— Aw, swell."

Wheeling around, he stalked off.

Devon hurried after him. "Wait."

He didn't slow down, forcing her almost to run to catch up with him. She snagged him by the sleeve and made him stop.

"Surely there are other repairs you can do in the meantime," she said. "Even some routine servicing—"

"Yeah, on Zero's nav unit for starters," he said bitterly.

Then he sighed, pulled in his chin, and scowled. "Okay. If I can't, I can't. I was trying to speed things up, make the repairs as efficient as possible."

"You always do a good job," Devon assured him.

"You don't think it's a good idea to hang around here too long, do you?" he asked, shooting her a glance she couldn't read.

"People need the rest," she said.

"But this cave," he said, glancing up and around uneasily, "I don't like it. Don't feel comfortable in it. And that dead city out there gives me the creeps."

"It is strange," she agreed. "Beautiful but—"

"There's something wrong about it."

"Like what?"

"I don't know. Maybe it's just alien." He shrugged, plainly uncomfortable with discussing his feelings. "I don't like True off playing in it."

"Maybe we shouldn't let the kids loose," she said thoughtfully. "If it's sacred ground to the Terrians, then—"

"Yeah, well, I don't know. I don't like treading on their toes, especially when—"

She waited for him to finish, but he didn't. "Especially what?"

"Forget it," he said gruffly. "You want something to do?"

She had to smile. Sooner or later Danziger always had a job for every member of the group. "Of course. How can I help?"

He almost smiled back. The anger had left his eyes at last, and he was the familiar, inscrutable Danziger again. "Come on," he said. "I'll teach you how to lubricate a wheel bearing."

She was following him up the ledge toward the exit when Uly's voice came faintly over her gear: "Mom! Help!"

Instantly alarmed, she stopped and turned around. "Uly?" she said anxiously. "What's wrong? Uly?"

There was a long pause, while a dozen conjectures flashed through her mind. Uly hurt. Uly in trouble. Uly—

"Mom, I'm okay," he said, his voice still faint and far away.

She frowned and tried boosting the channel, but it didn't seem to help. "Are you still out in the city?" she asked. "What's the matter? What's going on?"

"I'm okay," he said, his voice suddenly stronger and less frightened now. "I, uh, dropped my torch for a minute. It broke, but I've got a spare."

She sagged with relief, only then realizing how tense she'd become. Danziger was standing beside her, his eyes serious with concern.

"Okay, good," she said. "True okay?"

"Sure."

She nodded and gave Danziger a thumbs-up sign. He stopped frowning. "Why don't you two head back? Maybe there's been enough exploring for one day."

"Well, we're—"

"Uly, come back. You've done enough for now. You can go out again later."

He didn't answer.

She sighed, aware that Danziger's discipline with True worked better than hers with Uly. *So I've spoiled him,* she thought defensively. She frowned. "Uly!" she said sharply. "Did you hear what I said?"

"Okay," he said and cut off the channel.

She glanced at Danziger. "He dropped his torch and scared himself, but they're okay. They're coming back."

"Good," Danziger said. "I'd rather see them playing out in the daylight where it's— warmer."

She had the impression he'd almost said "safer," but she wasn't sure. "At least they're not hurt," she said, and he nodded.

"True can take care of herself," he said proudly. "I taught her to be self-reliant, not—" He broke off.

131

Devon frowned, stung by the criticism he hadn't said. "Not helpless," she said. "Not like Uly."

Danziger's gaze met hers then slid away. "I didn't say that."

She sighed. "Everyone thinks I protect him too much. But—"

"You love him. It's natural," he said. "The poor kid's been sick all his life."

"Yes, he has," she agreed fiercely. "All these years have been a struggle to keep him alive."

"But he's okay now," Danziger said gently. "Let him take a few risks. Let him fall a few times and find his own way out of the problem. He's a great kid, but he's got to stretch. Hanging around True's already done wonders for him."

"Hanging around True has gotten him into trouble," she retorted sharply, then held up her hands placatingly. "Okay, sorry. I didn't mean that."

"I'm just trying to point some things out to you," he said.

She nodded, struggling to put aside her worry. "I understand that. You don't know how hard it was to give him permission to go off today."

"Yes, I do. True's with him, remember?"

Devon nodded. That's what she was afraid of. Uly might be a little immature for his age sometimes, but True didn't know the meaning of the word "caution."

Danziger looked at the city and frowned. "The way he called you for help just now, all because he dropped his torch and scared himself . . . He's got to get beyond reactions like that."

"You're right," Devon agreed. "Julia keeps telling me the same thing. I'm trying." She swallowed. "I'll try harder. Maybe I should tell them they don't have to come back right now."

"No. True's supposed to help me this afternoon anyway.

132

She loves welding." He scowled. "Provided Morgan ever comes back with Zero so we can get to the job."

"He will," Devon said. "He can't smash down every wall in the city."

"He might. You know, sometimes I think Morgan doesn't have an ounce of sense."

"It doesn't pay to underestimate him," she said, "but sometimes I think you're right. If he doesn't come back soon, we'll go after him with torches and clubs."

Danziger grinned, and they walked out together.

In the heart of the city, however, True wasn't smiling and neither was Uly. They huddled next to each other at the foot of the mysterious wall, still breathless and shaken from their tumble down the incline. For a short time they'd been in complete darkness, but True had fished out the spare torch in her pack. Its light had brought back their confidence and helped them find the torches they'd dropped.

They weren't quite sure where they were at the moment, however. A roof over them concealed the sunlight that had been their navigational point. Now True was bent over the scanner's map, trying to get her bearings.

"We're right in the center of the city," she said.

"Yeah, we found the wall you were so interested in," Uly said. "If we hadn't been trying to get to it, we'd still be all right."

"You're the one who panicked," True snapped. "You're the baby who had to call your mom."

"Okay, okay," he said, hunching his shoulders. "I couldn't find you at first."

"You should have brought a spare torch like I did."

"Yeah, you're so perfect."

They glared at each other, then True sighed and glanced

at the ceiling overhead. "We've got to get out of here," she said.

Uly didn't argue. He crushed an insect with his boot heel and inched closer to True. They were both pretty scared and trying hard not to show it.

"We'll just climb out the same way we fell in," he said.

"I don't know. It's kind of steep."

"Otherwise we're boxed in. Do you want to sit here until the grown-ups come looking for us?"

"No!" She knew that would mean instant grounding. No more exploration. Period. Her dad would load her up with chores, and she wouldn't see any more of the city.

Uly got to his feet, crouching a little beneath the low ceiling. He shone his torch up the incline. It was like a chute and very steep the first five feet from the ground up. Then it sloped at a more gentle incline.

True also stood up, keeping her back hunched so she wouldn't bump her head until she reached the spot where the ceiling angled up parallel to the chute. It was hard not to feel buried alive down in here. But she told herself not to panic. They could get out of this, if they kept their cool. Her dad had always told her never to react blindly out of fear.

"Think about what you're trying to do and where you want to go," he would say.

She nodded to herself, reassured by his voice in her mind. Her elbow was aching where she'd banged it in the fall, but she ignored that.

"See that little bump up there?" Uly was saying. "If we can reach that, we can use it as a handhold."

"Move back and let me see if I can reach it."

They shifted places and True handed him her torch. Extending her arms up the wall, she jumped with all her might. Her fingers grazed the bump, and she slid down with a splattering of dust.

"Yeah, I can do it," she said. "Let me boost you up."

Uly gave her back her torch, which she clipped to her belt beside her canteen. He gripped his torch's strap in his teeth and put his foot into her laced hands.

She boosted him, grunting with the effort, and he scrambled upward on his belly, grabbing hold and kicking for momentum. She dodged his boot to keep it from smashing into her face, and yelled encouragement.

Uly squirmed furiously, reached the incline, and crawled up it rapidly without stopping once to look back. He vanished into the darkness above True, then she heard only silence.

She frowned, but his torchlight suddenly shone down into her face, blinding her.

"Made it!" Uly said triumphantly. "Okay, your turn."

She wished he'd waited halfway up to give her a hand, but he hadn't. She wasn't going to ask for his help now. After all, she was older and taller. She could do it herself.

"Keep your light steady so I can see," she said. "But stop shining it in my eyes."

He moved the light, and she blinked until her dazzled vision improved. She jumped, and missed. Jumped and missed. Jumped and missed.

Hot and out of breath, she paused a moment to rest. She'd done it easily the first time. Why couldn't she do it now?

"Come on!" Uly said. "What's taking you so long?"

"Just shut up and let me concentrate."

"If you can't get out, I'll go for help."

"Ulysses Adair, if you do that I'll never speak to you again!" she yelled angrily. "I can do it."

"Then do it. We've got to get back."

She bit back the reminder that without her help he'd still have been whining down here at the bottom with her. Sometimes he was such a dork. Clearing her mind, she focused on the handhold she wanted to grab, held her breath, and jumped.

Her fingers grazed it. She clamped them down hard and hung on although her arm felt as though it would rip from its socket. Her toes scrambled desperately at the wall, trying to scoot her up. Then her fingers slipped and she slid down, scraping her chin in the process.

Dust fogged around her, making her cough.

"What happened?" Uly asked anxiously.

She shook her hair out of her face and twisted her cap around so that the bill was at the back. "I slipped. Be quiet."

"You can't do it," he said, worry growing in his voice. "You're not tall enough to reach. I better go for help."

"Uly, no!"

"But—"

"I said no." She was angry now, angry and determined. "I'm going to do it."

"You can't—"

"I *can*!"

He fell silent.

She frowned, gathered herself, and jumped. Holding on, she swung her other arm up and grabbed on. The rock was worn and gave her little to hang onto, but she gritted her teeth and pulled herself up. Her arms shook with the effort, but she finally got her elbow hooked over the edge, then her heel. She nearly slipped and Uly cried out, but she hung on, sweating and grim. Inching herself up, she got her knee on the edge, then she was scrambling up the incline as rapidly as Uly had, not stopping until she threw herself bodily over the top.

She lay there in the dust, sobbing for air, adrenaline making her heart race.

Uly pounded her on the back. "You did it! You did it!"

"Yeah." She rolled over and started laughing with sheer relief. "I did."

Together they raced back out through the doorway into the street and stopped, breathing hard and looking back at the trap.

"Okay," True said, still finding it hard to catch her breath. "From now on we double-check everything. I have a feeling that's not the only trap in this place."

"Yeah," Uly said. "I think maybe they didn't like visitors."

"I still want to see what's over that wall. Those towers are beautiful inside it, and they haven't fallen in." True gazed at the beam of sunlight still shining down. "Maybe it's a palace."

"Has to be. That's why it's hidden behind a wall," Uly agreed. "That's why there are traps, to protect the king or whatever."

Then the eager light faded in his eyes. "We better get back, though, or my mom will be having a fit. I wish I hadn't called her."

"Me too," True said. "Otherwise we could have stayed until thirteen hundred hours. That's when Dad told me to be back."

Uly blew out his breath in disgust. "I guess I really messed it up."

"Naw," she said to cheer him up. "We can't get over the walls on our own anyway. We need to come up with a—"

"We could get rope and a grappling hook," Uly suggested.

"Forget it." True's arms still felt weak and trembly from the effort of pulling herself up. Tomorrow, she promised herself, she was going to start chinning exercises and build up her biceps. But there was no way she was going to climb a rope.

"Okay, I got a better idea."

"You *never* have a better idea."

Uly scowled. "Okay, Miss Smarty, how about my Mag-Lev chair?"

She blinked, impressed in spite of herself. "Why didn't I think of that? It's perfect."

"Sure. It can lift us right over the top. I'll tell Yale to break it out of the cargo hold for me."

"But will he?" True asked doubtfully. "Without a lot of questions? I mean, since you've gotten better, you haven't been using it."

Uly shrugged. "So I'll tell him I'm tired. It's my chair. I can use it if I want."

"Just don't lay on the sick act too thick," she warned him. "Or they won't let you out at all."

He nodded and glanced back at the tower. "Tomorrow we're going to see what's in there."

"And no telling anyone about what we found."

Uly crossed his heart solemnly and spit into his palm.

True did the same. They shook hands, smearing the spit to seal their pact, then ran like the wind to get back before the adults became suspicious, or worried, which came to about the same thing.

To their surprise, however, the adults thought using the Mag-Lev chair was an excellent idea.

"Much safer," Yale said.

"You won't waste so much time getting there and back," Devon told an astonished Uly.

"Sure," Danziger said to True. "I'll charge up the power supply and it'll be ready for you in the morning."

True and Uly exchanged puzzled looks of relief. Sometimes adults made no sense at all.

But being children, they knew better than to question good fortune when it fell into their laps. Questions often made parents reconsider, and that nearly always led to permission being taken back.

So Uly and True kept quiet. When Bess asked them the next morning what they'd found, they shrugged and said nothing much. She seemed disappointed that they wouldn't describe more, so Uly pulled the broken fragments of carving from his pack and showed them to her.

"But what are the houses like?" she asked. "What kind of things are inside them?"

"Nothing," he said.

She looked dubious, so True jumped in to explain. "Everything's empty. No furniture, no old pots, no pieces of things that have gotten broken. It's like no one ever lived here."

As she spoke, a shiver passed through her and she gazed past Bess at the city. Maybe that was it, she thought. Maybe no one ever moved in to start with. But why build a city if you weren't going to live in it?

Bess looked pensive. True knew that her dad and Morgan had had a big fight yesterday afternoon over Zero. This morning Morgan had already left again, earlier than anyone else was up. True couldn't help but worry that he'd also found the walled-off towers at the center of the city. Maybe he was getting to it first. She fidgeted, eager to be gone, but she couldn't go until her dad brought the Mag-Lev chair in from outside.

"Morgan said the same thing, that everything was empty," Bess was saying. "I guess they took everything when they left."

True frowned. She already knew her theory was the correct one. No matter how careful people were, they always left something behind by mistake. Or they discarded stuff they didn't want enough to move. True and her dad had changed quarters often enough for her to know that much.

So no one had ever been here, and maybe she was the first person to step into some of those buildings.

It gave her a strange, shivery feeling inside.

"Hey, True!" Uly called, running past. "Your dad's coming!"

"Gotta go." She flashed Bess a quick smile and jumped up.

When she turned around, she saw her father climb into the chair and activate the controls on its arm. The chair lifted into the air, hovering there on its anti-magnetic field, and then with a sudden swoop her father launched the chair off the ledge, riding it down like a rocket. Uly laughed and clapped his hands. True started laughing too, especially when her dad spiraled the chair and did some silly loops in the air before zigzagging to a landing near the camp. Love and pride came welling up inside her throat. He really was a neat father, the best.

She raced to him and grabbed his arm to give him a mock punch. He grinned down at her. "Your carriage awaits," he said, being silly, and swept her a bow.

She curtsied, going along with the game, and climbed in. "Thanks, Dad."

He tugged on a lock of her hair. "Sure, baby. You be careful out there, more than yesterday, okay?"

He'd been cool about the scrape on her chin and elbow, hadn't asked her too many questions. Unlike Uly's mom, who was *always* worrying, True's dad knew a kid had to get out and mess around, but still she could see concern in his eyes. He'd even suggested they should play outside, but it was too hot for that, and another herd of buffalo had changed his mind without her having to argue.

On impulse she threw her arms around his waist and gave him a hard hug. He was solid and muscular against her, and when he hugged her back she felt safe and secure.

140

"Sure, I'll be careful," she promised. She broke away first and raised the chair a few inches, hovering off the ground.

"Hey!" Uly said, reaching them and climbing on so hurriedly he made the chair dip to one side. "It's my chair. I'll do the driving."

Rolling her eyes, True surrendered the controls and glanced at her dad in time to see him smile. "What time do I have to be back?" she asked.

"Same as yesterday. Thirteen hundred hours. I'll have the tanks off by then since I have Zero's help today."

She nodded, eager to go but also looking forward to doing some welding. "Check," she said, imitating the drawl of pilots maneuvering their ships in and out of the station dock. "That's an affirmative from this ship. We copy all points from station control."

"Station control says green light," Danziger said, falling in with the game. "You have orbital clearance for departure."

Laughing, Uly hit the controls and they shot away, zooming across the cavern and leaving the lights of camp far behind. True's stomach dipped, and she screamed with laughter, hanging on tight with the wind whipping in her face.

"Where to first?" Uly asked. "What to play dive-bomb on old Morgan?"

True grinned, but she shook her head. Morgan had no sense of humor, not like the others. He'd probably run straight to her dad and complain. True sometimes wished her dad would just punch Morgan in the mouth and shut him up, but Dad never did. Not even yesterday when he was so mad.

"Let's head straight for the tower, the tall one under the light," she said. "I don't want to waste any time today.

141

There's got to be something neat inside it, unlike the rest of this place. I just know it."

"Affirmative," Uly said.

For fun, though, he lowered them just below the tops of the buildings and made them careen down the streets, whipping them around corners, bumping high over rooftops, only to swoop low again. Hanging on tightly, shrieking now and then with delight as her stomach flip-flopped, True made sure she kept her torch shining on high beam ahead of them. Uly was going just a little too fast for the visibility conditions, and she didn't want to crash into a wall.

Then, unexpectedly, they reached the center of the city and Uly put the chair on hover.

"No traps this time," he said. "No falling down any holes."

True nodded. She stared at the smooth, featureless wall curving away from them. Then her gaze went to the tall, slim tower, domed at the top and looking golden in the sunlight filtering down.

"Go," she said.

Uly pushed the controls, and the chair lifted straight up, higher and higher, until it was even with the top of the wall and they could finally see what lay hidden inside.

Chapter 10

• • • • • • • ●

Inside the walls, small trees of coral grew in oblong stone planters, glittering and twinkling in the sunlight that spread across the spacious courtyard. The inner space was marked off by the five towers, not one of which was the same either in height or in architecture. Until now they had seen nothing but white stone used by the mysterious builders, but the paving stones of the courtyard were laid in a gigantic star of black stone in the center, with its points stretching out to the edge of each tower. The black stone had been highly polished, until it almost looked liquid in the murky light. It was nonreflective, however, and True shivered when she looked at it too long.

"Don't land on the black part," she whispered.

Uly still had the chair hovering at the top of the wall. "I

won't," he whispered back. "Those trees look like skeletons, don't they?"

Until then she'd admired them, thinking they were pretty. Now she looked at them with a frown. "Maybe we shouldn't go in there."

Uly looked at her. "After Mom dropping hints that we should play outside today, and Yale wanting me to study some old holograms of ancient architecture? What are you, scared?"

She was. She felt as though she'd been dipped in the icy stream. But she wasn't going to admit it to Uly, not when he looked at her like that. She wasn't going to be the one to call this off.

"It's just strange, that's all," she told him.

"Yeah," Uly breathed, his eyes glowing. "Strange and weird. Really alien."

He lifted the chair over the top of the wall and brought it down cautiously, taking more care than usual. Finally he landed it near the wall between two of the coral trees. A weak little rectangle of sunlight shone across the white paving stones, and Uly parked the chair in that spot.

True ran her scanner over the place before she got off.

"Okay?" Uly asked. He looked around impatiently.

"Yeah. The scanner doesn't verify what this black stone is. Keeps shifting between metal and stone."

"Must be manufactured then," Uly said casually and walked toward the closest tower.

True hurried after him, taking care not to step on any of the black squares. "Manufactured how?" she asked. "Remember who lives on this planet."

"Boy, the Terrians sure forgot a lot of their old civilization, didn't they?" he said. "Or maybe this isn't a Terrian place at all."

"I think it is. Was," she said, looking around.

From this side the wall seemed to lean inward toward them, being widest at the base and narrow at the top. That was strange because outside the wall appeared to be straight up and down. She blinked, thinking about inversion physics, which she hadn't studied yet, and wondered why it would be used in a place like this.

"Not the Terrians we know," Uly said stubbornly. He slapped his hand against the side of the tower. "Looks brand new. Not like the other stuff in the rest of the city."

"Not like anything outside."

The tallest, slimmest tower stood directly beneath the shaft of sunlight. Its domed top glowed golden and smooth. There was not a window, not a door to be found on any side of its seamless walls. The tower to the right of it was squat and fat. The next one had an octagon shape with a flat roof. The next one stood four-square with a peaked roof and tiny slits for windows. The fifth one was extremely small at the base and flared wide at the top, like an upside-down vase. To True it looked as if a big gust of wind could knock that one over at any time.

"We can't get in the pretty one," Uly said in disgust. "There's no way in, unless you can figure it out."

True studied it for a moment and shook her head. "Too hard. Let's go look in some of the others."

They went to the short, fat tower, whose roof barely reached the top of the outer wall. Both of them jumped over the point of black stone and paused at the rounded doorway. A door of bronze metal was shut across it. Uly pushed on the door, and with a protesting screech it lowered like a drawbridge into the tower.

True shone her torch inside, checking for traps. But the floor looked solid. It was only sandy dirt, like what they'd seen outside, but oddly reassuring. The air was warm and didn't smell musty. She stepped inside cautiously, her fingers brushing past a small depression carved just inside the doorway.

The interior had been partitioned off with a small vestibule surrounding the entrance. The walls were a pale shade of blue that made True think of the sky. They seemed almost to move.

When she and Uly looked more closely, they saw that the walls were covered with a sort of delicate vine with narrow, tender leaves.

"How can anything grow down here without light?" True wondered aloud.

Uly hurried ahead. "Let's see what's through there."

She followed him through the open doorway beyond the vestibule, and they found themselves in a treasure house.

Stones cut in the shape of cubes of various heights and sizes stood as pedestals for chunks of gold and silver ore. The precious metals were almost pure, and would need very little refining. They had been stacked on every available surface inside the room, filling it. Some was even piled on the floor.

Uly picked up a piece of gold and hefted it. "Heavy."

"Of course. Gold's supposed to be."

He handed it to True, and she examined it closely with her torch, her fingers running over its surface constantly before she finally put it back on the pile from which Uly had taken it.

"Leave everything as it is," she said.

"Why?"

"Let's figure this place out first before we do anything to it," she said.

Uly frowned. "We could take just one apiece, couldn't we? Then we'd be rich."

"Your mom's already rich," True said repressively.

Uly sighed and put the ore back. Then he grinned. "Wouldn't old Morgan split a seam if he could see this?"

"Yeah." True grinned back at him. "He sure would."

"You going to tell him about it?" Uly asked.

She shook her head. "Never. This is our place. We found it. No one is going to know anything about it."

Uly nodded his head. "Right. Let's check out the rest of it."

They hurried outside. Behind them a stone shifted in one of the walls with a faint rain of dust, then moved no more.

The octagonal tower held what looked like all the furniture the rest of the city lacked. All three stories of it were crammed with oddly shaped chairs, chests, and little tables. Many of the pieces were inlaid with precious jewels that glittered in their torchlight. Dust and cobwebs lay across the things, and they found goblets stacked in chests, bowls in others, all fashioned from silver but untarnished. Some of the furniture, especially that made of wood and leather, had long since crumbled to dust. They wandered about, touching and looking, but taking nothing.

When they emerged from the octagonal tower, the door raised itself smoothly and silently behind them as though they had never entered.

"Cool," Uly said.

"Come on," True said, already hurrying to the next one.

Uly charged after her, and inadvertently stepped on some of the black stone. He yelled in startlement and jumped past it.

True whirled in fright. "What happened?"

"I stepped on it."

"Did it do anything? Did you feel anything?"

Both of them stared at the star as though they expected it to come alive. Uly shook his head to both questions. After a tense moment he walked over to the edge of the star and gingerly tapped it with his toe.

"Uly, don't!"

But nothing happened. Uly looked up. "There. We've been scared of it for no reason. It's just stone."

"It's *not* stone," True said stubbornly.

"An alloy then."

"Stone and metal don't make an alloy."

"Who says?"

"I do."

He made a face at her and swung away. "From now on I'm going to walk on it. See?"

He jumped on and off.

True watched him worriedly. "Don't," she said.

"Why not?"

"I don't know. Just a feeling I have."

He snorted and hurried past her to the next tower. Running up to it, he pushed on the door, but it did not lower as the others had. Instead it lifted straight up, swiftly. Startled, Uly toppled into the dark interior with a yelp.

True ran to him, expecting him to have fallen down another hole. But he was already rolling to his feet, unharmed. "Idiot," she murmured. "You can't make any assumptions about this place. Nothing works the way we expect it to. By now you ought to know that."

"Okay," he muttered in embarrassment, brushing himself off.

"I want to see how this door works," True said, moving off to one side. "Oh, look. It's a counterweight, perfectly balanced and . . ."

Her voice trailed off, and she stared overhead at the bottom of the door. In her torchlight its metal edge looked razor sharp. A groove in the threshold was designed to hold it, but if they were standing under it and it decided to come down . . .

She closed her mouth and shivered.

"What's the matter?" Uly demanded. He looked up and gripped her arm. "What's that? An axe?"

"More like a guillotine," True whispered.

"Wow. It could slice us in half just like that." Uly snapped his fingers and she jumped.

"Don't."

He moved on deeper into the room, but True stayed close to the door. Traps, she reminded herself. Traps everywhere. She had to remember that.

"Hey, look," Uly said. "These chests have scrolls on old paper stuff. No, it's more like a leather."

"Don't handle them too much," True warned him. "They look fragile."

Uly had already opened a leather case and shook one of the scrolls out. He unrolled it, the stiff fabric crackling in his hands. "It's got writing on it."

True joined him and shone her torch over it. "It looks like hieroglyphics."

"Yeah. True, we've got to take this back and show it to Yale. I'll bet he could decipher it."

"No."

"But—"

"I said no! We agreed not to take anything, remember?"

Uly's face twisted with disappointment. "Yeah, but this is one old moldy scroll, not important like the gold. How can it hurt?"

She took it from his hand, tearing it slightly in the process, and rolled it up. "They'll want to know where we got it."

"So we'll tell them one of the buildings."

"They'll want us to take them there."

"So we'll pretend we can't find it again."

She looked at him in exasperation. "When we have a scanner? Get real. You might fool your mom with that kind of act, but Dad will see through me in an instant."

"But—"

"We can't risk it, Uly. They'll want to come here, and then it won't be ours anymore. It'll be theirs. They'll see things like that door and they won't even let us come in. You know how they are."

"Yeah." Uly frowned, watching her put the scroll back in its case and lay it down. "But what if I show it to them later, after we're gone from here? That wouldn't hurt, would it?"

True hesitated. They'd found a lot of neat things so far. It would be a shame not to have some kind of souvenir. "Okay," she said finally. "But not until just before it's time to leave."

"I'll take it now and hide it."

She gripped his wrist to stop him from reaching for the scroll. "Too risky. Yale goes through your stuff. You'll never be able to hide it. We'll get it at the last minute."

"And what if we don't have time?"

"We'll make time," True said. "Come on. Let's keep looking around."

They approached the door cautiously. To True it appeared to be lower than it had been when they entered. She pushed Uly outside, hesitated, then jumped over the threshold with her heart pounding crazily. Not until she was outside, however, did the door lower slowly and smoothly. She heard the faint snick of steel against stone as the blade slid into its recess, and her mouth felt dry.

The fifth tower was the one that looked as if it were upside down. Its door also slid up, and although True checked carefully, she saw no evidence of a blade on the bottom of it. Once they stepped inside the narrow base, however, they found themselves looking at a tightly spiraled staircase of stone. The steps were narrow and extremely steep. Up and around they climbed, seemingly forever, until they came out in the broad top of the tower. One chamber occupied this floor, and the walls had been painted to represent scenes from a garden. The colors had faded, yet they remained beautiful. There was no roof, by design not decay, and True realized that had the cave not enclosed this place, this room would have been open to the sky. As it was, a meager amount of sunlight spread through the room, diffused and soft. It made the greens and blues in the paintings almost glow with life.

A chair, long since rotted, had once sat in the center of the room, as though for someone to sit in and gaze at leisure. True felt suddenly sad for the people who must have come here, looking at pictures of gardens, when in reality they lived in a dark cave. She realized that that was kind of how her life on the station had been: a place to live in the dark cave of space. And now she had come here to this planet, and could walk outdoors, and feel the wind and the sunshine, and breathe air that wasn't recycled. She'd always loved the station. She was happy there because she didn't know anything else. She'd been looking forward to getting home someday. Now she wasn't so sure she'd like it if she did go back. This planet had changed her, whether she had wanted it to or not.

She frowned.

"Let's go," Uly said. "This tower is boring."

She wanted to ask him if he appreciated the contrast between his former existence as an invalid and the free and happy life he lived now, but he was already hurrying down the staircase, and by the time they returned outside, the chance was lost.

Only the slim tower remained before them, mysterious and inaccessible.

"Okay, puzzle solver," Uly said. "Have you figured this one out yet?"

The scanner gave her no clues. She walked around and around the tower, still avoiding the black stones, although Uly tracked across any part of the courtyard now without fear.

"Without a door, how can we get in?" she asked aloud. "Maybe this one isn't so special."

"Don't be stupid," he retorted. "You know it's the most important one. The light wouldn't shine on it if it wasn't."

He was right.

She circled around its base one more time. Two shallow steps led up to the base all the way around. Finally she sat down on the top one with a sigh and propped her chin on her fists.

Uly sat down on his chair. "Hungry?"

"No." She frowned at the courtyard, aware that it had been designed in a particular way to convey some meaning. Concealment and illusion, she thought. Nothing is what it seems.

There had to be a door, only it wasn't where they expected a door to be. She gazed upward, but there were no doors higher up on the featureless sides of the tower. No windows, no openings of any kind.

Where were doors put? In walls, obviously. Sometimes in ceilings. Or maybe in the floor.

Jumping up excitedly, she went around the tower again. This time she noticed the oblong of sunlight on the ground. It was shining on a metal door, sun-colored and therefore hard to see. She stamped on it, hearing a hollow thud reverberating beneath her heel, and jumped back as it slid open.

"Got it!" she said triumphantly.

Uly hurried over while she descended the steps that led down into the ground. But before she'd gone down more than a half dozen, a terrible stench rolled up from below and engulfed her. It was horrible—the rotting, gruesome smell of decayed flesh, of death.

Gagging, she backpedaled, bumping into Uly, turning and pushing him out ahead of her. "Shut it!" she gasped, unable to breathe.

Outside she clawed at her throat, choking and coughing as Uly stamped to make the door slide shut again. The terrible smell stayed with her, however. It was in her lungs, filling her nostrils. She wanted to roll on the ground and scream to get away from it.

Uly gripped her shoulders. "True!" he said anxiously. "True!"

She shook her head wildly. "I . . . can't . . . breathe. I can't—"

Water splashed in her face, making her gasp and blink. The stench faded, and she was able to think again. Slowly she relaxed and wiped the water off her face.

Uly stood in front of her, his canteen in his hand. He looked scared. "You okay?" he said.

She nodded, feeling shaken. "Yeah, I think so. What was that?"

He clipped his empty canteen back on his belt. "I, uh, think it was someone's tomb."

"And we opened it. Ugh." She wrinkled her nose and shuddered. She was going to have nightmares over this. "After three thousand years it shouldn't stink anymore."

"I guess dead Terrians take longer to decay than humans do."

They stared at each other, and True didn't know whether to laugh or stay serious.

Uly frowned thoughtfully. "You know, all those history lessons from Yale . . . People, important people like kings and all, used to have themselves buried with their favorite things. Their money, their furniture, their chariots, and—"

"Their scrolls, their favorite gardens painted so they'd remember," True said, catching on.

They looked at each other, and the calm, cold air of the cave felt dead on their skin.

"Yeah," Uly went on. "And they used to hide their tombs so people wouldn't fine them and rob them. You know, 'cause there was so much gold and jewels there."

"Like we found," True said in a hushed voice.

He nodded. "I'll bet this whole city is just a cover-up for this tomb, to hide it."

"Maybe there're more courtyards like this, with towers." True looked around, hugging herself. "This whole place could be a graveyard."

"Yeah, like the Valley of Kings in old Egypt."

"That's why there're traps," True said.

"You know, you were right about us not taking anything," Uly said. "It would make us grave robbers."

She looked around. "I think we better go."

For once Uly didn't argue with her.

Far away on the opposite side of the city, Morgan finished prying away the last block of stone. He pushed it aside with a groan of fatigue and sank down, mopping his face with his sleeve. Yesterday had seen rapid progress, with Zero pulling down the blocks. He could supervise and give orders while the robot did all the work. But Danziger couldn't think of anything except the inside of an engine. The fool didn't even see the possibilities this place offered. Typical working-class mentality, Morgan thought with a sneer. If Danziger had any imagination, he wouldn't be a mechanic.

154

Still, the walled-up archway had been opened at last, and it now waited for him. Morgan drank from his canteen and shut off the big solar lamp he'd taken from camp.

The temple was a long, solid building of white stone. Its portico in the front was supported by columns similar to those at the cave entrance. The altar was a massive piece of solid stone, carved with a basin in the top that drained onto the floor and channeled away via a narrow groove that ran along the steps. Morgan didn't care about what might once have been sacrificed there.

Featureless doors stood beyond the altar, shutting off access to the rest of the temple. Morgan had studied enough ancient culture to know how these old religions worked. There were bound to be priest quarters inside, plus a storehouse, and a treasury to hold people's offerings. He had come to G889 because it offered him opportunities, but he'd never dreamed he'd stumble onto anything like this.

Grinning to himself, Morgan switched on his hand torch and stepped carefully through the hole. He shone his light around, keeping his eagerness under control, taking his time. There was no hurry, he kept telling himself. No hurry.

But he could feel his emotions surging, and he wanted to run. Ever since he'd realized what kind of place they'd stumbled onto, he'd felt a raging impatience to search and find. Bess had been teasing him about his gold fever, trying to talk him into quitting his search, but she'd stop that nonsense when he came back with his pockets full of riches.

The temple was the biggest of all he'd found, and the most impressive in scale and artistic form. It was also the only one sealed up. The others were simply roofs supported by columns, wide open and empty. People didn't lock up if they had nothing to steal, he told himself.

Chuckling, he shone his torch around the walls and found a series of steps leading down. Without hesitation he started down them, taking care not to slip on the damp stone. The air was cold and heavy with a dank, musty smell that made his nostrils wrinkle. Insects scurried ahead of him, fleeing the light.

Reaching the foot of the steps, he walked across uneven stone pavement, shining the torch at columns that supported the floor above him. A series of doorways ran along the far wall. Wooden doors, long since rotted, hung there in tatters on decayed hinges. He peered inside one of the cubicles on the other side of the doors, his heart beating fast.

Nothing. The room was empty.

The next held large clay jars.

The next was empty.

The last one, however, had a mound of something piled up beneath a rotting leather cover. His breath caught in his throat. He stood there a moment, too excited to move, then he pushed himself forward, step by step, not letting himself run, his palm sweaty around the torch.

This was it, he told himself. He'd found it.

The anticipation was almost better than the reality. He activated his private channel to Bess.

"Morgan," she said, sounding grateful to hear from him. "Are you all right?"

"Sure. Why shouldn't I be?"

"It's been hours since you left. I've been worried. Please don't shut off your headset again."

"No way," he said laughing. "Not now."

She hesitated. "You've found something?"

"Of course."

"What?" she asked excitedly. "Did you really find a treasure?"

"Oh, yeah. I'm beneath the big temple right now, and I'm about to put my hand on a very large pile of gold."

As he spoke, he grabbed a corner of the rotted leather and

yanked it back. Instead of gold pieces, however, he found the stacked skeletons of several Terrians. At least three skulls rolled toward him, disturbed when he pulled off the cover.

Horrified, Morgan stepped back hastily and stopped, breathing hard with shock.

"Morgan?" Bess called. "Tell me what you've found. At least transmit it over vid-feed so I can see too. Morgan?"

The stone beneath his feet shifted slightly. Frowning, he glanced down just as he heard a soft click. Suddenly the stone he'd been standing on was gone, and he went plummeting straight down before he had a chance to grab onto anything. One of the skulls rolled in after and fell with him.

He screamed.

Chapter 11

• • • • • • • ● ●

Devon and Danziger were outside, steadying the lines as Zero winched the second water tank off its fittings and swung it gently to the ground. Danziger had just grinned with satisfaction and stopped Zero when Bess's frantic voice came over Devon's gear.

"Devon, get everyone and come quickly!" she cried.

Devon waved at Danziger to stop and focused on what Bess was saying. "Don't go so fast," she said. "What's the matter? The children—"

"It's Morgan. Something's happened to him. Oh, God, please hurry!"

"Okay. Stay calm. We're coming now."

Switching off, she glanced at Danziger, but he'd heard and was already issuing orders to Zero to commence welding the tanks. Tossing down his tools, Danziger gestured to Baines and Walman, who were shooting craps on the ground.

"Look sharp," he told them. "There's trouble down in the cave. I may need you."

They nodded, putting their headsets back on, and he and Devon hurried inside.

By the time they reached the camp, they found Julia kitted up and armed. Alonzo was checking the charge on a solar lamp. Bess stood off to one side, holding a weapon. Her face was set and very pale.

Yale was on gear, calling Uly home. He switched off when he saw Devon. "The children are already on their way."

"Good," Devon said, keeping an anxious eye on Bess. "Stay with them."

"If there's trouble, you'd better take them to the surface," Danziger told him.

Yale's gaze moved to Devon, and she nodded agreement.

"Then I shall do so promptly," Yale told them.

Julia moved about briskly, handing a Mag-Pro and filled canteen to Devon. "He was on gear to Bess when it happened," she said. "The channel's still open, and I've linked through to his vitals. He seems to be unconscious, but we don't know whether he simply fell or was attacked."

Devon exchanged glances with Danziger, who frowned.

"We're waiting for that Mag-Lev chair," Julia continued. "I intend to use it to transport him back. His homing device is operational, and I've linked that to a scanner so we should be able to go straight to him."

"I say we go now," Bess said in a harsh voice. She took the scanner away from Julia and set out.

Alonzo shot Julia a look of disapproval and followed Bess.

"She's right," Devon told Julia. "We can't wait around

coolly and assess the situation from a distance. If he's hurt, we have to move now."

Julia looked chagrined. "But we'll need the chair—"

"The kids can bring it," Danziger said. "I'll tell True."

Julia fell into step beside Devon, frowning. "I'm sorry," she said. "Alonzo said I— Well, I wasn't trying to be unfeeling about this. I— It was the most efficient decision."

She broke off when Devon didn't respond. Devon quickened her pace to catch up with Bess and Alonzo, and Julia fell back with Danziger.

In minutes the chair came zipping up alongside them. Both True and Uly were big-eyed. "What's going on?" Uly demanded.

Devon stopped while the others went on. "Hop down. We need your chair."

Leaving the chair on hover, Uly scrambled off immediately and True followed suit.

"Did something happen to Morgan?" True asked.

"Yes," Devon said. She saw what leapt in their faces and added quickly, "We think he fell. We're going to rescue him now."

"We can help," True said.

"Yeah!" Uly chimed in.

Devon shook her head. "Thanks, but you two had better go outside with Yale."

"Stop trying to shove us out of the way like babies," Uly said indignantly. "We know more about this place than you do."

What he said caught her attention enough for her to overlook his rudeness. "Explain," she said, glancing from one face to the other. "What have you two been up to?"

"Exploring," True said, nudging him in the ribs.

Devon's suspicions increased. "Uly?"

He frowned, twisting about under her gaze. "The place is

tricky. There's a lot of places, uh, where, uh, you can fall."

Devon crossed her arms, frowning at both of them. "The lies and evasions can stop now. I want to know exactly what you mean."

True looked stubborn, as if hot pincers wouldn't drag an answer from her.

"Devon?" Danziger called.

She looked over her shoulder and saw the others getting too far ahead.

"You need us," True insisted. "If he's been poking around an old temple, then you really need us."

"Let us go, Mom," Uly said.

"No." She pointed at camp. "March. Now."

True and Uly exchanged a frustrated look.

"But we can tell you how to avoid the booby traps," Uly finally said.

Devon blinked. "What traps?"

"They're everywhere," he said. "You have to know what to look for."

"If you do, it's really safe," True said, watching her closely.

"Honest," Uly added.

Devon drew in a sharp breath, and her gaze wandered involuntarily to the silent ghost city. Who knew what was out there, lurking among those empty buildings? And her son had been playing among its security devices? She felt cold at the thought.

"We haven't gotten hurt," True said. "We've done fine. But there are places you can fall into and maybe not get out. That's probably what happened to Morgan. So you need us."

"All right," Devon conceded reluctantly. "But you two stay close. No going off on your own."

"We've been on our own for two days," True said.

Devon gave her a sharp look. "That was before this happened. Come on. Let's catch up."

Uly took the chair, and Devon and True trotted until they joined the others. Danziger didn't look pleased to see the children.

He glared at Devon. "Are you crazy? This isn't a hike. It—"

"They said the city is full of pitfalls and traps."

He blinked. "What kind?"

She shrugged. Both kids had melted away to the front of the group, with Julia, Bess, and Alonzo. "They were vague on that point."

Danziger snorted. "Are you sure this isn't something Uly made up?"

"Uly told and True was trying to keep it a secret," Devon said matter-of-factly, "so, no, I don't think it's made up."

He swore softly. "Some kind of primitive security devices, like falling stones, sinkholes, and the like?"

"Probably. They think Morgan fell into one of the traps, and they know how to avoid them. They seem to think we can't outwit the traps ourselves and need their help."

He raised his brows. "That's True for you. The world can't get along without her."

Devon was amused. "Well, it can't, can it?"

"No, not really." He glanced ahead at his daughter, and his gaze softened. "Not my world, anyway."

It took about forty-five minutes to hike around to the eastern side of the city and find the temple Morgan had been trying to crack. Alonzo's solar lamp threw out wide illumination that made their hand torches almost unnecessary.

As they wove through the narrow dark streets amid the silent buildings, Devon's skull prickled with uneasiness. Ghost city was right. This place was eerie, dead. The longer

163

they walked, the more she wanted to be far from it. How on earth could Uly and True stand to play in here?

Uly positioned his chair beside her. "Know what? There's nothing in any of these buildings."

She shot him a disbelieving glance as she stumbled over some rubble. "You can't possibly know that."

"Sure I can. Me and True got this whole place figured out."

"And?"

He frowned, glancing at True's back. "Uh, well, anyway you can go in any building you pick and you won't find a thing. Some of the buildings are fakes, just a front, see, not a whole structure. You have to really watch out for those."

"Why?"

"Sometimes there's a hole instead of the floor. And when it's so dark, you can't always see it in time."

Devon's frown deepened. "Is that how True scraped her chin yesterday, by falling down a hole?"

He fidgeted.

"Uly?"

"Gosh, Mom, don't make me rat on people."

Devon didn't relent. "Did she?"

"Uh, yeah."

Devon sighed. "What about you?"

"Me?" Uly said indignantly. "No way! I'm too smart to get caught like that. I—"

Under her steady gaze, his boasting wilted. Hanging his head, he nodded. "Yeah, me too."

"Oh, Uly. You could have been hurt."

"But we weren't. And we got out. We didn't have to call for help like old Morgan."

"Don't talk about him that way," she corrected automatically. "Your manners are getting sloppy, young man."

"Well, anyway, we didn't need any help."

"Here it is," Bess said from the head of the group.

They all stopped and stared at the temple. It was a very large, rectangular building, tall and rather grand. The columns were identical to those flanking the gateway outside, and they went all the way around the building itself. Broad steps led up to the portico, and Devon saw the altar Morgan had described. There was no door to be seen.

"Let's go around," Danziger suggested.

"Or split up," True said.

He gripped her shoulder. "No," he said grimly. "Until we know what we're facing, we stick together."

Uly parked the chair and hopped off.

With Danziger taking the lead, his rifle held ready, and Alonzo shining the lamp to light the way, they started around the side. Near the back, they found smashed stone and a toppled column that were clearly Zero's handiwork.

Tears stood in Bess's large eyes. Her face looked paler than ever.

Devon looked at the stone blocks that had been tumbled about carelessly, and the jagged hole torn in the wall. Morgan's crowbar lay where it had been tossed, and his canteen and jacket were beside it.

Bess seemed frozen in place. Finally Devon took the scanner from her hand and swept the area.

"He's inside," she reported. "But not on this level."

Danziger was peering through the hole. "There are steps."

"Right," Julia said. She started forward, but True blocked her path.

"Wait," she said. "All of you can't go down there."

"True—" Danziger started.

"Wait, Dad. I know what I'm talking about. If this temple is a really important place, then it's got a lot of tricky things to protect it."

"Protect it from what?" Bess asked blankly. She wiped her eyes.

"Looters," True said.

All the adults flinched. Bess began to cry. "He didn't mean anything by it. He just wanted to—"

She couldn't finish. Devon put an arm around her and hugged her close.

"Meanwhile we have an injured man down," Julia said. "It's important we reach him quickly."

"Right," Danziger said. "Okay, Alonzo and I will go in—"

True and Julia protested at the same time.

"He could be in shock," Julia said. "I don't like what I'm getting on his vitals. Delay could be—"

"Take my place then," Alonzo said. He handed her the lamp.

"Dad, I've got to go," True said.

"True—" He broke off and sighed. "Okay, lead on."

With a satisfied nod, True adjusted her cap and switched on her torch. She climbed through the hole and started down the steps. Julia went next, and Danziger followed.

Alonzo perched himself at the top of the steps, gazing down, his Mag-Pro in his hand.

Bess looked at Devon. She was calmer now, but her eyes still looked bruised with worry. "I'm not staying out here," she said. "He's hurt. I've got to help him."

"Bess, Julia is a very capable doctor—"

"I'm not going to do nothing but wait," Bess said angrily. "If it were your husband, would you?"

Devon winced. "No," she agreed. "I wouldn't." She glanced at Uly, who was prowling along the side of the building. "Uly? Can you avoid the traps as well as True?"

He straightened up importantly. "Of course. I know what to watch for."

Devon gestured at the hole. "Then lead us inside."

Alonzo scrambled out of the way. They filed past him, and he brought up the rear, picking up the crowbar with his free hand and looking alert for trouble.

The steps leading down were damp and steep. Devon steadied herself with a hand on the wall. Moisture seeped through the rough stone. Her fingers felt chilled from touching it. Again she had an almost overpowering sensation of immense, weighty stone pressing down upon her. A little dizzy from it, she stopped and blinked the feeling away. Odd, but she'd never suffered from claustrophobia before. Still, if this place wouldn't bring it on, she didn't know what would.

At the base of the steps, they found the first group standing in a knot while True scouted ahead. The girl was moving close to the wall, her torch aimed not at the cubicles lining the opposite wall, but the floor. Everyone stood silently, but Danziger's knuckles were white on his rifle as he watched his daughter.

Devon had to grab Bess's wrist to keep her from pushing on after True.

"But we've got to hurry," she said. "He's hurt. He needs—"

"I don't see anything," True reported from the end of the broad hallway. She peered into the last cubicle and backed out hastily. Her face was pasty white.

Danziger stepped forward. "True—"

She glanced at him, her eyes enormous in her face. "It's—"

Devon heard nothing, but True suddenly jumped aside as though she'd been stung. The flagstone she'd been standing on seemed to vanish, and True teetered a moment on the brink of falling in before she caught her balance and backed away to safety.

"He's down there," she said, panting.

Danziger and Alonzo sprang forward. Alonzo peered into the hole, and Danziger looked into the cubicle. Devon heard his gasp all the way down the hallway.

"What's in there?" she called.

"You don't want to know."

"Hey, quick!" Alonzo said. "It's closing."

Danziger grabbed what looked like a stick and thrust it into the hole, wedging it so the stone wouldn't close completely.

As she drew closer, Devon saw that the stick was a femur. She swallowed hard, feeling queasy.

"He said he'd found it," Bess was saying. "He must have been standing right there—"

"What he found were Terrian skeletons," Danziger said grimly. "He probably backed out of there just like True did, and stopped right on this stone."

"Then it fell," True said, having regained her voice now.

Uly suddenly poked Devon in the arm. "Mom, don't stand there."

Devon quickly jumped aside, feeling a little foolish and scared as well. "Why? I can't see anything."

"Look at the way the stones are laid," he explained. "Perfect and flat. But that one's not. And that one's not. And this one you were standing on isn't either. I'd be suspicious of them."

"See," True said, "a lot of things work on balance and counterweights. It's pretty neat, actually, except if someone gets hurt."

Danziger said, "If that's the case, you could probably walk quickly across this floor in safety. It's when you stand for a few seconds in one spot that your weight activates the lever."

Alonzo was prying on the bone they'd wedged between

the stones. "If so," he grunted, "how do we get this one open, eh?"

"Not that way," Danziger pointed out. "You're working against the counterweight. Apply pressure on this side, and it should swing open."

He pushed on the opposite side of the stone, and it vanished again. This close, Devon heard only the faintest scrape of stone against stone. She shifted her feet nervously, wary of the entire floor now.

Alonzo put down the crowbar and started paying out rope from his pack. Danziger knotted a loop into the end and Alonzo wrapped the rope loosely around a column. Then, leaning his weight against the rope, he lowered Danziger down the hole while Devon shone light into it.

"I'm down!" Danziger called.

"Do you see him?" Bess asked.

There was a pause. "No."

Bess pressed her hands to her mouth, and Devon and Julia frowned at each other. Devon looked at the scanner. It still indicated that Morgan was right below them.

"I don't get this," she said. "John, look for his headset."

"Looking now," he replied. "I don't find it."

"There's another level down," True said suddenly. "Has to be. Nothing here is ever as it seems. I'm going down."

"True, no—" Danziger said in alarm, but she was already swinging down the rope.

Alonzo grunted as he jumped to counterbalance her weight. "She's going too fast. She'll—"

A muffled cry from True made them crowd around the hole again. "Is she all right?" Julia called.

Danziger's reply came over their gear: "Yeah, but she's got some rope burns."

"Stand by. I'm coming down," Julia said.

She waited while Alonzo hauled the rope back up, then

she put her foot into the loop. Holding on, she let Alonzo lower her. Devon watched the rope sliding over the stone, hoping it wouldn't fray.

"Down safe," Julia reported.

Bess stood up. "I'm going next."

Alonzo frowned in concern. "Are you—"

"Don't argue," she said in a voice that was uncharacteristically stern. "All of you, stop protecting me."

In silence, he lowered her. Then he and Devon looked at each other. Devon sighed. "If we've got to make a longer search, we'd better stay together. Uly, you're next."

The boy went down, then Devon. She watched anxiously while up above Alonzo tied the rope securely to the column and wedged the stone open more firmly with the femur. Telling them to stand well back, he dropped the crowbar down through the hole. It landed with a bounce, metal ringing loudly off the stone floor. Then Alonzo lowered himself down the rope, fist over fist, and landed lightly on the balls of his feet.

He pulled an emergency flare out of his pack and opened it. A greenish, sputtering light filled the space, which looked identical to the room they'd just left: another rectangular passageway, with more cubicles on one side. He positioned the flare next to the rope and caught up.

"Okay, watch out where you're stepping," Danziger cautioned them. "Remember the uneven flagstones are the—"

"No, Dad," True broke in. "Probably not this time. Things are never the same."

Uneasy looks passed among the adults. Alonzo wiped sweat from his forehead. "Great," he muttered.

"There's no door, no way out," Bess said, looking around. "Where could he be?"

Devon checked the scanner. Morgan's homing device still beeped clearly and steadily. "Down," she said.

The floor was a regular pattern of stone squares, all smooth and even. Devon crossed it warily, keeping an eye on Uly. She wished she'd never brought him here.

"We'll fan out, check those cubicles," Danziger said. "Everyone, take care."

True was already ahead of everyone else, though. She hurried along, shining her torch into each cubicle. It was Devon who noticed that she wasn't looking at any contents that might be inside them, however; she was looking at the thresholds.

She had started at the farthest one and worked her way back. In the middle, she froze. "Here it is," she said. "At least I think so. Uly?"

The boy joined her and looked. Devon started in their direction, but then Uly picked up a loose brick that was too heavy for him and, grunting with the effort, his thin arms wavering, tossed it inside the cubicle. "Uly, no!" Devon cried, but she was too late to stop him.

She heard a hollow thump and then stone, and a shriek in protest.

"Dad, quick!" True shouted.

Danziger sprang forward and caught the door before it could close again. Alonzo helped him force it open. They wedged it in place with the crowbar and shone the torches down.

"I see him," Danziger said.

Julia moved forward, but Bess reached the hole first. "Where?" she said anxiously.

Gently but firmly Danziger pushed her back. "Give us time to get to him first. Please."

She nodded, anxiety twisting her face, but she stayed out of the way.

"Did the brick Uly threw land on him?" Devon asked.

Uly's mouth fell open and he turned bright red as though finally realizing the possible consequences of what he'd done. Right then, however, Devon was too worried to scold him. That would come later, if and when they got out of here safely.

"No, I don't think so," Danziger replied.

Devon shot Bess and Julia a glance of mingled relief and apology while Uly squirmed in embarrassment.

Turning back to the mechanic, Devon asked, "Do we need more rope?"

"Nope. It looks like a chute," Danziger said. "We can slide down."

Uly and True exchanged knowing looks. They nodded to each other.

"I'll go first," Danziger said. "Then I'll stand by to spot the next person down. Julia, I think."

She nodded, her face calm and purposeful. She tapped him on the shoulder. "Go."

Danziger swung himself into the chute and slid in a cloud of dust and a rattle of pebbles. Devon heard him land.

True leaned over. "Okay, Dad?"

"Yeah. Come on."

Julia climbed over and vanished. More dust fogged up from the hole.

"She's down," Danziger said. "Everybody stay put while she—"

In the distance something slammed.

Devon glanced up and around with a frown. "What was that?" she asked.

They all shook their heads. True and Uly whispered to each other.

Moving closer to the hole, Devon peered down the chute. In the torchlight she could see a cramped space below. Most of it was filled by a mound of what looked like dried mud. The surface of the mound was cracked, and it vaguely resembled the shape of a person, squatting, with arms outstretched. There was a head, its features long since blurred with age. Morgan's crumpled body lay across it where he had obviously fallen. *Like a sacrifice laid out on an altar,* Devon thought before she drove the unwelcome thought from her mind.

Puzzled, she drew back and glanced around at the area where they were waiting. Morgan couldn't have fallen through this chute and landed on the altar.

"Uly, True," she said, a warning in her voice, "don't prowl around. There's another way down."

Bess and Alonzo were intent on watching what Danziger and Julia were doing below. They paid Devon no attention, but the children froze in place like startled animals.

"What do you mean?" True demanded.

Devon explained, and True began to frown.

"Okay," she said, nodding. "That makes sense." She glanced at the ceiling above them. "Like there's another trapdoor right above us here, so whoever comes through it will go down the chute we found."

Devon also glanced up. She had that creepy feeling again, as if they needed to get out of here. There was something ominous about the place. Morgan and his treasure, she thought. Morgan and his foolishness.

Julia's voice came over her gear: "He's unconscious from a blow to the head; probably hit it when he fell. There's concussion and some pressure, but nothing as severe as I feared. I'm checking him now for broken bones, and then we're going to move him off this thing."

True's head snapped up. She gripped Devon's arm. "No," she whispered, wide-eyed. "They can't move him."

"Of course they can," Devon said, not understanding her. "That's what we came for—"

"No! I told you, things here are balanced. When you move something, the wrong thing, you change that. Then you get into trouble."

"We're not taking anything that belongs here," Devon said, trying to calm her down. "All we want is Morgan."

"Okay," True said, but she still looked worried. She backed up, her gaze sweeping the ceiling, and stood near the flare and the rope that was their way out. "Okay."

Uly crowded against Devon, and she put her hand on his shoulder. Something in the distance slammed again. And again. Each time it was louder, closer, like a succession of doors shutting.

True whirled around. "Quick!" she cried. "We have to get out of here."

"Why—"

"Quick! Quick!" True reached for the rope and started climbing despite her injured hands, but she didn't get very far before the stone overhead swung shut, snapping the bone Alonzo had wedged there. The cracking, splintering sound made Devon jump. The rope was cut, and True fell hard.

Devon ran to her, scooped her up. True looked pale and shaken. She was trying not to cry with pain, but she gave Devon a shove. "Move!" she gasped. "Not safe."

Uly tugged at Devon's sleeve. "Mom, come on."

"Devon!" Alonzo yelled urgently.

Devon whirled around with True in her arms and saw him beckoning. Bess was already going down the chute.

"It's shutting," he said in a gasp, straining to hold it. "Get through before we're cut off from the others."

Devon hesitated only a second. There would be time later to sort out what was happening and why. Right now she had to act.

She pushed Uly to get him started. The boy ran to Alonzo and scrambled past him. Uly was already sliding down by the time Devon and True got there.

"You next," Devon said to True.

The girl nodded and launched herself.

Alonzo grunted. Cords were straining in his neck. His face was dripping with sweat as he strained to hold the door open.

"Hurry," he whispered.

"What about you?"

"Hurry!"

She couldn't argue with him, couldn't help him. He was using his legs, those recently healed legs, to brace himself against the stone. It ground closer, and he groaned with effort.

Devon slipped past him and didn't check to see if the way beneath her was clear before she was sliding down the stone chute, her clothing ripping on its abrasive surface, her heart pounding with fright.

Then she was pitched forward and falling. She landed awkwardly, rolled, and came upright, feeling shaken and dizzy, but basically intact.

Danziger helped her up without even looking at her. They were all crowded together around the crude mud altar, in a space too small to hold them, staring up at the ceiling, where Alonzo still held the stone open.

"Come on!" Danziger called to him.

Julia looked white. Bess was kneeling over Morgan. Uly and True stared up, open-mouthed and frightened.

"He can't do it," Devon said. "He's holding the stone with his feet. If he lets go and drops, I'm not sure how fast the stone will move."

"It could cut him in—" Julia stopped herself.

"You can do it, Solace!" Danziger called out encouragement. "Tuck and drop all at the same time. Now, man! Come on!"

There was another slam of stone, closer and loud enough to make all of them jump. Then Alonzo was hurtling down, sending dust and gravel ahead of him. Danziger caught him and kept him from landing in a heap.

He was all in one piece, but unsteady on his feet. His forehead was bleeding, and his dark eyes weren't quite focused.

Danziger sat him down, propping him against a wall, and Julia went to work.

"Just a little bump on the head," she said, her voice less steady than her hands as she sprayed a bandage over the cut and cleaned the blood from his face.

"Why is he shaking like that?" True asked.

Danziger caught her around the shoulders and pulled her close. "Adrenaline. It overloads the system and has to work its way out."

Alonzo blinked and came round. His eyes focused, and he gave Julia a smile. She sat back on her haunches. "He'll be fine," she said in relief. Her gaze moved to Morgan, who was still unconscious. "They both will. But how are we going to get out of here?"

Chapter 12

• • • • • • • ●

Thirst pulled Devon away from the camp and sent her walking toward the stream. She climbed the rocks beside the little waterfall, hearing its muted roar and feeling the spray of moisture on her face. The cavern was lit throughout by a soft even glow, and that alone told her she was dreaming. *I don't have time to dream,* she thought. *We're in trouble. We have to find a way to solve our problem.* But the dream didn't stop, and she kept climbing until she reached the still, deep pool.

She knelt beside the water. In this light it no longer looked black as it had before. Instead it was now clear. She could see to the bottom. Thirst made her bend down. She needed a drink desperately. She cupped her hand in the cold water, but it dribbled through her fingers, and she was able to swallow nothing. Frustrated, she crouched lower and put her face to it.

She drank long and deep, feeling its cold goodness refresh her. The worry nagging at the back of her mind did not seem quite as strong now. Satisfied, she raised herself up and smiled at her reflection in the water.

It rippled on the surface, and then changed. Her face became a Terrian face.

"No!" she gasped, but long, powerful arms reached up from the water and gripped her before she could dodge back.

"No!" she screamed, struggling, but it was already pulling her down, down deep beneath the icy surface of the water.

Devon struggled awake with a wrench. "No," she gasped, shuddering. "No!"

The powerful hands were still gripping her arms. She fought them and felt herself being shaken.

"Devon, wake up. Devon!"

The vividness of the dream faded, and she found herself blinking into Danziger's concerned face. She sagged with relief and lifted her hands. He released her.

"Bad one?" he asked.

She nodded.

"Any Terrians contact you in your dream?"

There was hope in the question. She glanced around and saw that most of the others were still sleeping.

She frowned and pushed back her hair. "Not the way you mean. One was trying to drown me."

"It didn't speak?"

"No."

Danziger frowned. "Damn, I guess I was hoping for some help. Why, I don't know. We did defy them by coming here."

"We *had* to come," Devon said. "We couldn't just die out there in the desert."

"I know," he said soothingly. "No one's blaming you. Don't blame yourself."

She wiped her face again and settled back with her shoulders against the wall. They'd been in this small room for hours, unable to find a way out. Little True had exhausted herself, working on the puzzle. Now she slept on the floor, her face streaked with dirt. Uly was curled up beside her.

They'd tried calling for help, but there'd been no reply from Yale, Baines, or Walman. Either their signal had been cut off, or something had happened to the three men as well. So much for rescuing Morgan, Devon thought bleakly.

Danziger sat beside her in silence. They all knew their time was limited if they didn't find a way out soon. The kids had some energy bars in their packs, which they'd already eaten. None of the adults had brought food with them. Everyone had canteens, but the water wouldn't last long.

Then what? Devon wondered. She didn't want to think about a long, lingering death trapped down here.

They weren't dead yet. There had to be a way out.

"If you can't sleep either," she said softly, "let's work on this."

"Sure," Danziger said. "What angle haven't we already hashed out a dozen times over?"

"Nothing is as it seems," Devon said, quoting True. "Most things about this place seem to be an illusion."

"So?" he said. "We're not really in a room beneath the ground, I guess. And we're not really trapped."

She looked at him with exasperation, and he sighed. "Sorry," he muttered. "I don't like no-option situations."

"So we make options," she said.

He visibly pulled himself together. "Right."

"We're people of the modern world," she said. "We're at least as smart as the ancients who built this place. Even True and Uly have outsmarted them so far."

"True and Uly wouldn't have gotten themselves trapped down here," he said wryly.

"Probably not," she said with a little smile. "God knows what they've encountered on their own."

"Yeah, just thinking about that is one reason I can't sleep." He rubbed his jaw and frowned. "So nothing is as it seems."

"Everything is an illusion," she repeated.

She stared hard at the altar. It was extremely crude and primitive in comparison to what they'd seen of the rest of the temple. She had the feeling it was much older. Maybe it was the original altar, maybe not.

"True said we shouldn't touch anything, shouldn't pick anything up, or move it."

"Okay, so Morgan moved the skeletons, and he fell through the hole."

"Yes. And you and Julia moved him off the altar, and all the trapdoors closed."

"So if we put something back on the altar?" he suggested.

"True already climbed on it, and nothing happened," Devon said with a frown. "I don't think that's the answer. There wasn't anything lying on it before Morgan happened along."

Danziger nodded and pressed his thumbs together thoughtfully. "So what was the existing condition of this room before any of us came along?"

"Empty," she said.

He frowned.

She looked around, seeking inspiration, and her gaze fastened on the solar lamp, which had been turned down to a muted glow. "Dark," she said.

"What?"

"It was dark in here. We've had lights blazing since we arrived."

"Oh, come on, Devon. The Terrians don't have light-sensitive technology. They couldn't—"

"But the coral," she said.

"What?"

"The coral we found when we first ventured into the caves. It has some chemical property that senses and reflects light. Maybe there's something like that in here."

"But there's no coral growing in here."

"No, but there's mud. Or a mudlike substance."

Scrambling to her feet, she picked her way over the sleepers and switched off the solar lamp.

Absolute darkness fell over them. Blind, Devon stood in place, waiting, listening to the sounds of steady breathing.

Then she saw it, the faintest, palest glow of reflective light possible, coming from the altar. It faded to darkness almost before she could register it. At the opposite end of the room, she heard stone sliding aside.

"That's it," she said sharply.

Someone stirred at her feet, with a mumbled inquiry.

"Wake up!" Devon said in a loud voice. "Everyone, wake up. Don't switch on any lights. No lights!"

They stirred around her, bewildered in the dark.

"Mom?" Uly called.

"I'm here, son," she replied. "Keep still, but don't turn on your torch."

"Devon," Danziger said, his voice containing muffled excitement. "I think I heard—"

"You did," she said quickly. "It opened. We've found our way out."

"Where?" True asked over a yawn.

"One of the walls. We'll have to hunt for it."

"In the dark?" Bess said.

"Yes!" Devon replied sharply. "Light will close it. Don't ask how. Let's concentrate on getting out of here."

"But it's not the way we came in," Bess said.

"I know. But it's the best we've got."

"We have to be careful," True said. "Without light, we can't see the next trap."

"Once we're out of this room, we'll turn on the torches," Devon said. "Now, everyone grab onto the next person, and don't let go. We're the blind leading the blind in here. John, you search for it. No one else. Just John. We'll make a human chain. That way we won't lose anyone."

"What about Morgan?" Bess asked. "He's still unconscious."

"I'll carry him," Alonzo offered. "If I can find him."

"Okay, everyone stay still until Alonzo does that," Devon ordered.

They waited, listening in the dark, while Alonzo fumbled around.

"Got him," he said finally.

"One patient shouldn't carry the other," Julia said. "Someone else—"

"I'm doing it," Alonzo said sharply. "Let Devon stay in charge. She's doing a damned good job."

For a moment there was only abashed silence. Devon frowned, wishing he hadn't stepped on Julia quite so hard.

"Everyone ready?" she finally asked.

They gave her an affirmative.

"Go, John. Find the door."

They groped along, helpless in the darkness, relying on the uncertain senses of sound and touch, each hanging on desperately to the next person. This creeping progress seemed to go on forever, until Devon wanted to scream with impatience, then finally Danziger grunted.

"Found it," he said.

Everyone started talking at once.

"Hang on!" Devon said over the babble. "Don't relax yet. Let's get out, one at a time."

"Be careful, Dad," came True's voice.

"I am," he replied. "It's a passageway, uh, feels kind of crumbly, like dirt for walls instead of stone. The ground is solid. It's dirt too."

"Each person say your name as you go over the threshold," Devon said. "That way we'll be sure we haven't left anyone."

"Danziger."

"Uly."

"Bess."

"Alonzo and Morgan."

"Julia."

"True."

"Devon."

As she bumped out into the damp, cool passageway, feeling mud seep through the knees of her pants, Devon breathed a sigh of relief. All accounted for. All safely outside.

"We made it," she announced. "Everyone stay on the floor. I'm going to switch on my torch. Just one."

"Wait!" True called.

Devon froze with her finger on the switch. "What's wrong?"

"We should check the ceiling," True said. "Just in case."

"Check it for what?" Danziger said.

"Sharp blades."

Startled, Devon nearly blurted out a question, but she held it back. Now was not the time. "Okay. John, do you think if you stand up, you can feel it?"

"Hang on." There was a pause, then his voice came out of

the darkness. "Yes, this is a pretty tight passageway. Low ceiling. In fact it's about ten centimeters above the top of my head. Watch out, people, I'm going to step on you."

He came back from the head of the line, bumping along, evoking muffled grunts when he trod on fingers or feet, or bumped into someone. Partway along, he stopped.

"What is it?" Devon asked. Her hearing was more attuned now. She heard him hiss under his breath. "John?"

"Cut myself," he said calmly.

"How bad?" Julia asked.

"Don't know. I'm going to nudge someone with my foot. Who is it?"

"Me," Julia said.

"Okay, move forward. Everyone in front of Julia do the same. Not too far, just so we can all get on the other side of this blade."

"It's like a guillotine," Uly said. "Whoosh—"

"Uly, quiet." Devon reprimanded him sharply. Her nerves were stretched tightly enough without him adding to the tension.

The person ahead of her crawled forward, and she followed until her shoulder brushed against Danziger's leg.

"Okay, we're past it," she told him.

"Right. I'm going in the other direction, just to be extra sure."

He fumbled his way forward again, and when he reached the head of the line he hadn't found any more blades in the ceiling.

"Okay, Devon. It's the best I can do."

Holding her breath and saying a little prayer, she switched on her torch.

Nothing happened.

She was so tense it took her several seconds to comprehend that. Then she sagged in relief and wiped the sweat off her brow. "Whew," she said, glancing back at their pale faces. A few smiles began to appear as they looked at one another. "I thought it would—"

The open door to the chamber they'd left slid shut with a sudden thud, and the blade overhead came down with a snick of steel against stone. It landed less than a meter from Devon, a sheet of metal without feature that blocked the passageway completely.

She stared at it, too shocked to breathe for a moment. Then she swallowed and rose to her knees unsteadily.

Julia was already up and pushing her way ahead to Danziger. Devon glimpsed crimson blood running down his hand, then Julia was spraying it with antibacterial agents and coagulents. She bandaged it swiftly, holding her torch in her teeth.

Alonzo said, "I do not like this place."

"Bess," True asked, "where did you leave my koba? If he's by himself, he'll be scared and—"

"He's okay," Bess reassured her. "I left him with Yale."

"Oh."

"Come on," Danziger broke in grimly. "We have a lot more to be concerned about than one baby koba. Let's keep going while the way seems clear."

They hastened along as fast as caution would allow, everyone keeping a sharp watch for danger. Alonzo and Bess supported Morgan between them. He moaned a little, as though he might be regaining consciousness, but then he passed out again.

Devon frowned at him. She didn't want him hurt, but indirectly he'd gotten them all into this mess, and she couldn't help but feel angry. If he'd helped with the repairs instead of wandering off . . .

But it did no good to think that now. They had to keep going. They had to get out.

They walked maybe a klick or two before the passageway broadened into a chamber. Four equally crude tunnels branched off from it.

"Now what?" Danziger asked, looking back at Devon.

She pushed her way to the front, frowning tiredly.

"Oh, no," Julia said suddenly. "I can't believe I was so stupid."

"What's wrong?" Devon asked her.

Julia handed over the scanner. "I was so busy linking it to Morgan's homer, I forgot to take a directional. We have no reference point now."

Bess frowned at the tunnels in dismay. "So we'll have to guess which way to go, and we could guess wrong."

"I'm sorry," Julia said, red-faced. "It was a stupid mistake. One of the first things we were taught at the orientation for this expedition, and I—"

"Forget it," Danziger told her. "Anyone would have done the same. I didn't think about it either."

"But you weren't in charge of the scanner," Julia said, not ready to stop blaming herself. "I should have thought—"

"Relax," True said. She pulled out a scanner from her pack and switched it on.

Devon frowned and hurried to her. "What are you doing with that? You aren't supposed to play with these."

"We weren't playing with them," True said in irritation. "We didn't want to get lost, so I had it do a schematic of the city. We have a map, see?"

Devon's annoyance vanished. She looked at True with approval. "Very smart."

"Yeah, only that's the surface. I don't know about under here."

"I can change it over," Devon said, taking the scanner from True. She referenced it and took a directional, then punched in commands to link the directional with the grid already established. Then she had the instrument scan. In seconds a new schematic, of the underground tunnels, appeared.

"Okay," Alonzo said, peering over her shoulder. "You have a reference point as here. That is a problem. If we fail to come out, this is the only place we can definitely return to without getting lost."

Devon sighed. "We need the camp as our reference. Except we can head west."

"But look," Alonzo said, pointing at the tiny screen. "The tunnels do not run that direction. They go primarily this way, here in the center of the city. It looks like we have no choice but to follow them, even if they do seem to go in the wrong direction."

"Don't worry," True said. "We know where the tunnels are going."

"Where?" Devon asked her. "How? Explain."

True and Uly exchanged looks, almost as though they were reluctant to tell. "Well, it was going to be our secret," True began.

"Forget that nonsense," Danziger said impatiently. "You tell us what you know."

"We found the heart of the city," she said, avoiding his gaze. "There's a walled-off place, with five towers. It's right where the sunlight comes in from the surface. It's the only real part of the city, the only part that matters. We think," she faltered, as they all stared at her. "Anyway, most of these tunnels are going to it. If we can get there, we won't be lost. Uly and I can get back to the camp from the towers easily."

Devon met Danziger's gaze. He raised his brows, and she shook her head.

"You two," she said, but she didn't have any energy to scold them. Instead she bent over the screen and chose the one tunnel that took a direct route to the central section. "The second from the left," she said, pointing at one of the tunnels before them.

Bess wrinkled her nose at it. "That's the smallest one. We can't even stand upright to go in."

"I don't know about you, but I want to get out of here as quickly as possible," Julia said.

Bess nodded, sighing and glancing worriedly at Morgan.

"We'll take turns with him," Danziger told her, slinging him over his shoulder. "Devon? Lead the way."

"No," Alonzo said swiftly, stepping ahead of her. "I will lead the way. She is the navigator. She is more important. If my head is sliced off, we will still have her to follow."

And he ducked into the tunnel, his torch shining into the darkness as though to drive it back for the rest of them. Looking back once, to count the rest of them, Devon followed. In silence the others entered one by one, ducking low as they came after her.

Chapter 13

• • • • • • • ●

They seemed to trudge forever. They kept a constant watch for traps, but encountered none. It was impossible for Devon to relax. She developed a superstition that as soon as she let down her guard they would be attacked by some kind of vicious device.

Worst of all, there was no person, no individual, behind the danger. Everything was impersonal, set ready long, long ago, and therefore much more alien. They could not reason with the devices. They could not appeal. All they could do was watch and hope their wits and reflexes would be quick enough to save them.

Ahead, the tunnel curved, after having gone fairly straight for a long time. Devon tensed, wary of any change in the conditions. Before her, Alonzo suddenly stopped.

"Oh, no," he breathed.

At once the knot in the pit of her stomach tightened. "What?" she demanded, peering over his shoulder.

The tunnel had been blocked by a cave-in. Crumbly dirt stood mounded from floor to ceiling.

"It's not fresh," Alonzo observed. He walked forward to touch it. "Very soft. Should be easy to dig through. Hold my torch."

"Wait," Danziger said, pushing his way forward from the rear. He slid Morgan off his shoulder and eased him to the ground.

Morgan was finally awake, blinking as though the torch-light hurt his eyes. He mumbled a question, and Bess knelt beside him, soothing him and wiping his brow with a damp cloth.

"I have to dig," Danziger said.

"Sure, you can help," Alonzo said, but Danziger shook his head.

"It's my job."

Alonzo patted his shoulder. "You are tired, old man," he said, grinning a little at his own joke. He was close to thirty years older than Danziger, although he looked younger. "We will all dig."

"No, I have to do it."

"Why?" Devon asked. "Explain."

Danziger scowled, shoving his hands deep into his pockets. "It's a dream I had, of being buried alive by the Terrians."

Alonzo blinked. "They talked to you?"

"No. Just started pouring dirt over me. You're still the one they talk to, Solace." Danziger rubbed his stubbled jaw. "I've dreamed the same thing twice since we've been here. I figure it's important."

"Yes, like my water dream," Devon said.

"Well," Alonzo mused, frowning over it. "Perhaps if you

are to be buried alive, you had better stay far away from this. It could be a warning, not an order."

"Oh, for God's sake," Morgan said irritably from the floor. "What's all this mumbo jumbo about dreams and the like? It's just an ordinary cave-in."

Devon, Danziger, and Alonzo looked at one another.

"He's better," Danziger said without joy.

"Sounds like the Morgan we hear every day," Alonzo said.

Devon frowned at both of them. "Let's start digging."

They took turns at the job, using their hands. The ones not digging shoved the dirt down the tunnel, spreading it out to get rid of it.

Soon they hit rock, and the work got harder. Danziger was hampered by his cut hand, but he worked steadily beside Alonzo, both of them sweating freely. Then, when they rested, Devon and Bess took a turn at moving the stones, one at a time. True and Uly grabbed the small pieces of rubble, trying to help without getting in the way. Julia guarded Morgan, refusing to let him take a turn.

"The men are tired of carrying you," she told him sternly. "So sit tight and rest. When we get through this you can walk on your own steam."

Alonzo and Danziger took over again. After a few minutes, Danziger backed up and said, "I think we're through."

Devon's head snapped up. She joined him, shining her torch through the narrow opening at the top of the pile. "I can crawl through that," she said, then eyed his broad shoulders. "Can you?"

He nodded wearily. "Tight fit, but I'll go through. I don't think we'd better shift any more stones or the rest of this roof may come down on us."

Devon glanced uneasily at the top of the tunnel and shut her eyes. *Don't think about it,* she told herself.

"Right," she said.

"I go first," Alonzo broke in. "Then Devon. Then the kids."

"I'll go last," Danziger said.

Anxiety flashed across True's smudged face. She hurried over to stand beside him. "Why do you have to be last?" she asked.

"Because I'm the biggest, and I might make it fall in."

"Then I'm waiting to go with you."

"True—"

"No, Dad." She looked up at him, and after a moment he nodded, a muscle clenching in his jaw. He patted her shoulder without a word.

"We go," Alonzo said.

He gave all of them a quick, bright glance. Almost as though he were bidding them good-bye, Devon thought with a shiver. Then he climbed gingerly up the pile of rubble, some of the stones shifting a bit beneath his weight.

He eeled through and vanished except for the soles of his boots. Then even they were gone.

"I'm through," he called.

Everyone heaved a sigh of relief.

"All right, Devon," Danziger said. He gave her a little smile for luck.

She walked toward the rubble, then pulled Uly to her. "You first."

"But—"

"Go on," she said, giving him a little push.

He flashed her an anxious look, but she kept her expression confident, hiding the nervousness she felt while he scrambled up and wriggled through easily.

Then it was her turn. She seemed to feel every stone

shifting under her. The hole looked tiny as she crawled into it. Stone brushed her back and dug painfully into her stomach. She kicked through, trying not to dislodge anything, then slithered down the other side faster than she meant to and rolled up against Alonzo's feet.

He grinned down at her. "I have always wanted a strong career woman at my feet," he teased and helped her up.

"I think you've got the wrong one," Devon said, pulling her hand away and slapping dirt off her clothing.

He sighed and tilted his head. "Unfortunately, you are correct. Next!"

Finally they were all through except True and her father. By then Alonzo was frowning worriedly at a crack in the ceiling. "We have dislodged too much support, I think," he muttered under his breath.

Devon held her torch trained on the opening, not breathing as she waited for True to come through.

"Be very careful, little one," Alonzo coached her.

Devon could hear cautious scrabbling on the rocks, then she saw the top of True's head.

"Good, good, you are doing very well. No sudden movements, no stopping."

True was panting, either from fear or exertion, but finally she crept through. A little patter of dust rained down on her from above.

They all looked up.

Devon bit her lip in worry. Danziger was the biggest. He should have gone through first.

"How's it holding on that side?" the mechanic's calm voice asked.

"It's looking shaky," Alonzo replied.

"Over here too."

"We could shift around, try to shore it up," Alonzo offered.

"Nope. Wouldn't do any good. We don't have the right leverage to provide real support. Hey, Bess?"

She looked up. "Yes, John?"

"You say a little prayer, okay?"

"I will."

A lump filled Devon's throat. Her eyes were suddenly stinging. True gave a little gasp, and Devon put her arm around the girl. Tensely they listened to John climbing on the other side.

"The rocks are shifting too much," True whispered. "He's too heavy for it."

More dust rained down from the ceiling.

Alonzo gestured, serious and intent now. "Julia, get everyone back."

Slowly, unwillingly, they shuffled a few paces away.

Alonzo's head whipped around. He scowled. "Way back! Up the tunnel. Quickly!"

"You move away too," Julia said, her voice not as cool as usual.

The rock overhead creaked.

"I mean it, Alonzo," she said.

They gazed at each other long and hard.

Then he blinked and shook his head. "A brave man should not die alone."

"And what good is it if you both are—"

He gestured fiercely. "Get back! All of you."

He retreated too, but only a few steps.

Devon moved the others back, taking over from Julia.

True argued with her, but Devon was firm. She didn't want the child to be a witness to whatever might happen.

"How far are we going?" True asked.

Devon faced all of them, urging them on, listening to Alonzo calling out encouragement to Danziger.

"Farther back," she said firmly, until they reached a second curve in the tunnel. "Now—"

A low rumble filled the air. She smelled the dust before she turned around and saw it.

A choking mass of rock and dirt rained down, caving in the tunnel where Alonzo had stood. One of the torches went out, and suddenly they were crouching in the dim, dust-fogged light that remained, unable to hear anything except the terrible sound of the cave-in, unable to see.

"No!" True screamed. "Daddy!"

She tried to rush forward, and Devon barely caught her. The child fought, screaming and flailing. Devon hung on grimly.

"No, True," she said over and over, her own heart breaking. "No, True. You can't."

"Daddy!" True sobbed.

Then the rumble stopped, and all they heard was each other coughing in the dust. True stood there, stiff in Devon's hold, her lip trembling.

"I'm sorry," Devon said. She tried to pull True against her, but the child wanted no comfort.

She wrenched away. "Leave me alone!" she yelled and ran toward the cave-in.

Up on the surface, Yale paced back and forth slowly, worriedly, with the young koba on his shoulder. Out beyond the overhang, starlight shone down over the valley. No herds had come through since early in the day. The perpetual dust had begun to settle, and the world seemed peaceful. But Yale's heart was not peaceful. He had lost contact with the rescue party hours ago, and he had not been able to raise them.

Their homing devices were working. On the scanners, at least, they were all together and moving through the city.

But although Yale had finally ventured all the way around to the eastern side with Zero in tow and found the temple that Morgan and Zero had desecrated, had found the abandoned Mag-Lev chair, had found the canteen, jacket, and crowbar, he had not been able to find his friends. Nor had he been able to discover where they had gone. He could not imagine why they would choose to go exploring with an injured man. That was an illogical line of action, and Devon was nothing if not a logical woman. There must be another reason, and trying to determine what it might be made him most uneasy.

Yale paced slowly back and forth. The two remaining colonists had no comfort to offer. Since arrival, they had steadfastly refused to go inside the cave for very long, saying it gave them the creeps. Now they were bedded down on the hard ground beside the equipment that had been repaired in Danziger's absence, both snoring softly while Yale stood a lone sentinel, listening to the distant howl of the scavengers, and worried.

Zero was his only company, and he had switched the robot off down at the camp, taking no pleasure in his perpetual cheerfulness.

A movement on the slopes across the valley caught Yale's attention. Frowning, he focused his artificial eye in that direction, adjusting for night vision. He zoomed in and saw three Grendlers squatting in a row, clutching their staffs and gesturing quietly among themselves. One blew a soft melody that reached out across the plains. Yale listened, but no answer came in return.

Yale frowned. Usually Grendlers traveled alone. He had seldom seen them in groups, and he could not imagine what this trio was up to. They had the aspect of spectators, and that thought was disquieting.

He had lived many, many years in the service of Devon

Adair, had known her since she was Uly's age. He had always been grateful to her for her kindness, for her treating him like a human being instead of merely a cyborg tutor. He had not always approved of the choices she made or of the way she'd driven herself in recent years in the course of her career, but she was a bright, successful woman, someone he was proud of, and he knew she had done much to make his life better than it might have been.

If not for her, he would have been cast out of service long ago. He thought of the possibilities and shuddered. No, he had much to be grateful for when it came to Devon and Uly Adair, two people he loved very much.

He stood alone in the night and felt helpless, felt as though they needed him. Yet he could not offer them rescue or assistance. His brows knitted together in frustration. What good were his knowledge implants? What good knowledge of any kind, when action was needed?

Pulling at his goatee, he decided the Grendlers across the valley posed no threat, and he pulled his gaze away from them. He started pacing again, then abruptly turned and walked into the cave. His infrared vision switched on automatically, and he negotiated his way through the dark without difficulty.

He did not know what to do, did not know what he could do. But do something he must.

Reaching the camp, which he had packed up and stacked ready to be loaded just in case, he sorted through Uly's things briefly, searching for a clue that would help him. He found fragments of stone carving, taken from the rubble. Yale turned them over in his hands, smiling faintly to himself. The boy had a good eye and an incisive mind. He had not yet learned discipline, and his imagination was wayward, but given time Yale had great hopes for his scholastic ability.

Yet the carvings did not tell him where to find Uly.

To calm himself, he went through the boy's last lesson. Terrible mistakes, sloppy logic, really—he must strive to make Uly concentrate more. Then, crammed in the middle of arithmetic problems, Yale found a drawing. At first he was annoyed. This was evidence of Uly's daydreaming when he should be paying attention.

But something about the drawing caught Yale's eye, and he studied it more closely. It was a castle of sorts, fitted with five poorly drawn towers.

Then Yale frowned and reconsidered: perhaps not badly drawn, perhaps accurately drawn. Each tower had a different architectural style, yet there was something alien, something calculated, about the hodgepodge. A black star was centered among them, and each tower sat on one of its points. Something about the star disturbed Yale. He thought he remembered a reference of some kind, if he could access his deep memory.

But that involved time, and he was suddenly filled with a nameless fear he could not rationalize away.

Putting away Uly's belongings, he folded the drawing carefully and placed it in his pocket, then he made a schematic of the city and located its center. In abstract mode, he quickly perceived that the supposed maze of narrow streets all led sooner or later to that one central area.

That then was where he would go.

Another part of his mind, the conditioned part, sneered at his fears. What good was a blind course of action, chosen at random and based solely on intuition? He'd been wiped. He was not supposed to have intuition.

He was not supposed to love either, or remember.

But he did.

On the ground the koba ran back and forth, as though

searching for True. Then it stopped and gazed up at Yale in appeal. He lifted it to his shoulder with a sigh.

Grimly Yale told himself he was still a man and he would do everything he could to help his friends, no matter how illogical or foolish. There was something atmospheric about the cavern, something sinister about the city despite its silent beauty. Perhaps that caused his fancies; perhaps not. He knew he did not imagine that his friends were in danger.

He activated Zero. "Come," he told the robot. "We're going back to the city."

Zero swiveled his head and flexed his arms in a standard series of self-checks. "This time we'll be successful in searching," he announced, his voice booming off the stones.

Yale set out, with Zero lumbering steadily beside him. He hoped they would be successful. He sincerely hoped so.

Chapter 14

· · · · · ● ● ●

Down in the tunnel, running through the thick dust, True collided with Alonzo, who was staggering and coughing. They clung to each other a moment, then True twisted away from him.

"Dad!" she called. "Dad!"

Alonzo gestured at Devon, who was following. "Hurry. We might be able to dig him out."

"There's time," Julia said grimly, almost treading on Devon's heels. "If we're quick enough before he suffocates."

The tunnel wasn't big enough for everyone to help. True was already on her hands and knees, digging furiously like a dog by the time Devon reached her. Devon started digging, and Alonzo pulled True out of the way to take her place.

"Hurry," True said. "You've got to hurry."

"They're doing their best," Julia told her.

But True couldn't be still. "Why don't we have Zero here?" she moaned. "He could get Dad out."

Devon's fingers were soon bleeding, abraded by the rocks and dirt, but she didn't stop. She couldn't bear to think of Danziger buried alive, just as he'd dreamed.

The thought made a cold sweat break out over here. Prophetic dreams? she wondered. And me? Am I to drown?

"I've got him," Alonzo said.

Devon paused a moment in sheer disbelief. She'd expected them to find him at the bottom, not in the middle of the heap. But Alonzo was brushing dirt off a sleeve. Then he unearthed a hand. He gripped it and grinned.

"He squeezed back. He's alive! Dig, Devon. Dig with all you've got."

They went at it furiously, exposing Danziger's head first and turning it so he could breathe. His face was coated with dirt, nicked and scratched in several places. Alonzo blew dirt out of his nostrils and tried to clean it off his shut eyelids.

"Never mind that," Julia ordered. "Move aside."

Devon and Alonzo scrambled back, and the doctor bent over Danziger. True stood stiff and frozen, and Devon gave her little pats on the shoulder. "He's got to make it. He's got to make it!" She didn't think True even heard her.

The rest of them were silent, afraid to utter a sound.

Julia ripped Danziger's exposed sleeve and gave him an injection. "That should kick start his breathing again." She monitored him for several seconds, frowning severely, then blinked.

Glancing up, her eyes met Devon's and she gave a little nod. "I've got him back."

True started sobbing, and Devon held her tight. "He's

okay, honey," she said, brushing True's hair out of her face. "He's okay."

Morgan squeezed forward, moving slowly and stiffly, as though he hurt all over, and helped Alonzo dig Danziger out. They dragged him farther into the safer part of the tunnel, and Julia bent over him again.

After a short time, his eyes fluttered open and he began coughing. "What—"

Julia gripped his arm. "Don't talk yet," she said in a clear, firm voice. "You're safe. You survived the cave-in."

He frowned, looking bewildered as though he didn't remember. "True is—"

"I'm here, Dad," True said, kneeling on the other side of him. She brushed some dirt off his face. "I'm so glad you're okay."

The confusion cleared from his eyes, and he gave her a smile. "You look kind of funny. You been crying?"

She sniffed and wiped her face quickly. "No, not at all."

"That's my girl."

He sat up with Alonzo's help and let Julia check him again.

"You'll live," she said dryly. "Skull like iron. Headache?"

He rubbed his temple. "Yeah."

"Good. That'll remind you you're alive, which you're lucky to be. If you experience any dizziness, let me know at once."

She pushed herself to her feet and looked at Devon. "He'll be fine. Just shaken a little."

"Can we go on?" Devon asked.

"Don't see why not." Julia's brows pulled together. "But let's hope we don't go through that again."

Slowly they formed a file and started walking again. Now it was Devon who led the way, and Alonzo who brought up the rear. True walked beside her dad, keeping a steady arm around him and glancing up at him constantly, as though afraid he would vanish at any moment.

They'd been incredibly lucky so far, Devon realized— lucky that they still had everyone, lucky that no one had gotten killed.

She fought off a growing sense of weariness. The tension and constant need to stay alert were taking their toll. Time had lost all meaning, and yet surely they were getting near the heart of the city. This tunnel had to end sometime.

Ahead it curved, the ceiling rising so that her hair no longer brushed it. Warily, hoping no trap awaited her, she rounded the corner and stopped. Ahead of her the tunnel dead-ended.

It was not a cave-in this time. The tunnel simply stopped. Somehow she had chosen the wrong one. Now they were indeed trapped, for going back was impossible.

Overwhelmed, Devon stepped back. Dismay filled her, making her eyes sting. She couldn't have made a mistake. She'd checked the scanner. This tunnel went all the way through. She was sure of it.

Then anger overcame her disappointment. She struck the wall with her scratched fist. "You can't stop!" she yelled at it. "You can't stop!"

The others crowded behind her, passing back the bad news.

"Devon," someone said.

But she wasn't listening. She saw a rock projecting from the bottom of the wall and kicked it hard with her boot toe. "I won't let it end here!" she shouted.

The ground under her feet shifted. She jumped back, bumping into Bess, who was directly behind her, and stared.

Where she'd been standing was now an opening about a half meter square. Water glistened in the torchlight, lapping softly at the edge of the opening as though stirred by currents below.

Fear seized Devon's heart. She felt suddenly cold and clammy and had to lean against the wall for support.

No, she thought. *I can't go through that.* Not after the dream.

But that was it, she realized. That was what the dream had been telling her, showing her. Would she drown, or would she come out on the other side?

"What is it?" someone at the rear asked. "Water? What does that mean?"

"Devon?" It was Danziger's voice, and suddenly he was there, bruised and still caked with dirt. He gripped her arm. "Your dream?" he asked softly.

She opened her eyes and nodded. For once she didn't mind letting him see her fear and vulnerability. "I can't," she whispered.

He nodded. "It's got to be a way out. A way under the wall."

"Maybe," she said, wanting to believe him but unable to. "It could be another trap. What if there's no way out?"

"You decide," he said. "We can go back, try another route. I think we can dig through the bad spot and get back through. God knows, this has been devious enough for us not to trust anything."

She said nothing. He backed away and issued orders for a rest.

Everyone sat down in the tunnel, their faces tired and haggard in the torchlight.

Uly came and sat beside Devon. "Mom?" he asked quietly.

She looked up at him, giving him her full attention.

"You don't really think that's the way out, do you?"

"I'm not sure," she said wearily, avoiding looking at the

water. Until now she'd seen water only as a precious resource, the means of survival in the desert. She'd been focused on preserving it, locating more. She'd been so smug when they'd found the stream in the cavern. And now . . . now she was deathly afraid of it, afraid of dying in it.

"How far will we have to hold our breath under water?" Uly asked.

"I don't know."

She thought of currents, swift and strong. She gripped her son's frail hand and thought of the bone-chilling cold. Uly couldn't swim a river. He didn't have his breathing apparatus with him, and his lungs were far from strong.

Yet, to go back, to give up now, when they'd come this far . . . She felt a cool hand on her brow and opened her eyes again to find Julia beside her.

Julia checked her pulse and ran a monitor over her. Devon frowned. "I'm fine."

"You're exhausted. We all need food and rest."

"We don't have any food," Devon said. "And we may not have time to rest. How long until this opening closes again?"

Julia's cool eyes appraised her. "You honestly think this is the way out?"

"Yes," Devon said, surprising herself. "I do."

"I am an excellent swimmer," Alonzo said. "I shall go first."

For a moment Devon was relieved. Alonzo often seemed all charm and irresponsibility, but he was always there in a pinch, ready when needed. He could go in, see if the way was open or blocked, and let them know.

And who's the leader of this group? asked a little voice inside her head. *Who's the person who drummed up this*

206

colony, who promoted it, who recruited it, who promised people a better life and a better vision of the future?

Going first wasn't Alonzo's job. It was hers. And she had to find the strength to do it. She had to find the strength in herself to let Uly risk the same danger. The Terrians had warned her once to let Uly grow. Julia and Danziger had repeatedly told her the same thing. She bit her lip and fought not to cry.

Gathering Uly close, she kissed his cheek, then she got to her feet and adjusted the fit of her headset.

"Wait," Danziger said in alarm. "You can't wear that underwater. The feedback will shock you. Take it off and keep it in your pocket."

Devon's fears came raging back. "No gear?" she asked in a voice smaller than she intended.

He shook his head, understanding what was racing through her mind. It was the last lifeline she had. Now she had to really go on blind trust, something she'd never been good at. She was always the planner, the one who double-checked every detail, who followed up on tasks she delegated to her assistants, who demanded perfection in herself. Blind trust in a dream? She must be crazy.

Slowly, her hands shaking, she took off the headset and zipped it away in her pocket. "I'll call when I get through," she said.

They all stared at her, their eyes large and worried in the torchlight. She fought not to look too long at Uly, not to let him see her fear. *Be strong so he can be strong,* she told herself.

Turning her back to them, she eased herself feet first into the water. Its icy coldness was a shock. She hesitated, half-in and half-out, shivering already. Then she drew a deep breath and let herself drop beneath the surface.

For a moment she could see nothing, then her vision

adjusted to the watery infraction of her torch's light. It was muted, casting hardly any illumination at all. She pushed herself forward against the current with a strong kick and sailed into a wall.

Panic clutched her throat. So it *was* a trap. She could feel tiny bubbles of air escaping from the corners of her mouth. Her breath had almost run out. Frantically, she started to turn back, but her hand brushed something.

She paused and shone the torch over it. A carved stone handhold shimmered before her, fastened to the wall, as solid as age itself.

She gripped it, as her body floated sideways with the current that swept by, and shone her torch up the wall. She saw another hold and kicked up to it. Above her was another. She reached it, and her head broke the surface.

Gasping and shuddering, she pulled herself out and rolled over onto solid ground. Her torchlight bounced wildly off the walls, but she didn't bother to look at her surroundings. Shivering violently, chilled to the bone, she took out her headset and put it on.

Adjusting the mike, she called them. "Danziger? Can you hear me? Danziger—"

"I hear you," he replied, his voice very faint but understandable. She thought she heard him laugh. "You've alive, kid. You didn't drown."

"No!" She laughed back. Suddenly she felt invigorated and refreshed. She didn't care how cold she was. Slinging her wet hair out of her eyes, she said, "The current is strong, but make sure everyone faces the end of the tunnel when they go down. They should kick forward, and that will take them to a wall. There are stone handholds, three of them, that lead up to the surface."

"Affirmative," he said faintly, and cut off.

Scooting back, she wrung water from her hair, then took

off her jacket and did the same to it before emptying her boots. By then Julia was coming up, her hair unbound and sleek to her head. She seemed calm about the whole experience and climbed out as though she went swimming in dangerous underground streams every day of her life.

Bess came next, sputtering and shivering. They helped her out, and she shook herself like a dog. "Golly!" she said, wiping her face and blinking around. "Golly!"

Uly followed her, then True. Bess and Julia set to work, shucking the children out of their wet clothes and rubbing their arms and legs briskly to help keep their circulation going. Uly looked blue to the lips, but he was hopping up and down excitedly.

"Boy, that was something," he said, his teeth chattering.

"We need a fire," Julia said and proceeded to make one out of a fuel cap in her pack. She pulled the kids over to it and started them drying.

By then Morgan had arrived. He still looked far from well, but his personality was coming back. "Looks like one more goose chase," he said, glancing around. Then his interest perked up. "Hey, not a bad place."

It was a handsome room. The ceiling vaulted far overhead, and the walls were pale, polished agate, inset with different bands of color. Agate steps led up and away from the water to an area where benches of the same stone were located. The place had the look of a spa, or a bathhouse, and was extremely elegant.

"Maybe—" Morgan began.

Devon glared at him, and he had the grace to look down. "We've had enough treasure hunting, don't you think?" she said.

Bess shot her a look of reproach. "Don't scold him. He's learned his lesson."

"I hope so," Devon said.

By then Danziger was climbing out. Water streamed off his clothes, leaving muddy streaks on the stone landing. "One way to get clean," he grunted and hurried to the fire.

Alonzo came last, wheezing and sputtering. Julia gave him a hand out, and he spun her around in a smooth dip and kissed her on the cheek before releasing her. She scowled, her face bright red, and retreated.

Devon grinned at him. "I thought you were the expert swimmer."

He pounded water from his ears. "So I breathed in when I should have breathed out."

They toasted themselves by the tiny chemical fire until it finally petered out. By then their clothes were mostly dry and they'd all stopped shivering.

Confidence flowed back into Devon. She felt more than ready to go on. Circling the room, she found no visible door and paused. Her eyes went to True.

"Okay, where's the door this time?" Devon asked.

True was looking worried. Almost reluctantly she pointed at the far side of the room. "Over there. But maybe we should spend the rest of the night here. Maybe we should go on tomorrow, and tackle things when we're rested."

"What things?" Devon asked suspiciously.

"We've been gone about fifteen hours," Danziger said, checking his chron. "The night is just about gone."

"Yeah, but I mean we shouldn't face things in the dark. We should wait until daylight."

Danziger frowned at her in concern. "True, we're in a cave, remember? It's always dark, no matter what time it is."

"I know that," she said impatiently. "But the tower stands under the crack in the ceiling. Daylight *does* come in right at this spot. It would be better to—"

"Better to do what?" Devon said sharply. "True? Uly?"

Both children frowned and clammed up.

She advanced on them. "It's time to explain exactly what you know about this place."

Uly dug his fists into his pockets and scuffed his toe on the floor. True pulled the brim of her cap low over her eyes.

"I mean it," Devon said. "No more games. No more keeping secrets. We're not out of danger yet, are we?"

"No," True said in a small voice. "We're probably in the most dangerous spot of all."

Chapter 15

• • • • • • • ●

For a moment there was no sound at all in the chamber, then Devon walked forward and pulled up True's cap so she could see the girl's eyes.

"Explain."

True frowned and glanced at Uly, and it was he who answered: "Well, Mom, this city is really a big fake."

"A fake?" Devon repeated in puzzlement. "What do you mean?"

"We prowled through a lot of the buildings and we didn't find anything. I mean, they were empty. I told you it was weird."

"Yes, I remember," she said, nodding. "Go on."

"So then True and I found this place and we used the Mag-Lev chair to get over the walls."

"Ah," Danziger murmured.

Uly shot him a nervous look. "Yeah, and anyway, we started poking around in the five towers, and they had lots of neat stuff, like gold ore in one, plates and cups and furniture in another, scrolls in the third—"

"Uly, are you sure?" Devon asked, unable to believe him.

He looked wounded. "Mom, I am *not* making this up."

"The fourth tower had paintings," True put in.

Devon blinked. "Paintings? Of what?"

True shrugged. "Gardens and stuff like that. And one old chair in the middle, like it was there for someone to sit and look at them. Then the last tower was hardest to open."

"Yeah," Uly broke in. "We figured it had the really important stuff in it."

"But when we got it open, it was like a tomb or something." True's eyes darkened with unpleasant memory. "We didn't go in."

"No," Uly said, shaking his head. "It stank really bad."

"But after thousands of years," Julia began, then stopped with a frown.

"Nothing is like we expect it to be," True said. "After that, we figured out this city is a fake. Not real at all. It was just built around these towers and the courtyard to hide them."

Their theory intrigued Devon. "Why?" she asked.

"Well," True hesitated, "we think the inner city is a tomb."

"Yeah," Uly said, nodding. "For a king."

"Terrians don't have kings," Morgan said.

Both children looked at him with scorn.

"They might have three thousand years ago," Uly told him. "Anyway, who says the Terrians built this place?"

"They did," Alonzo said with quiet authority.

Everyone swung around to look at him, and he shrugged.

"Dreams," he said laconically. "Little conversations. They did."

"Anything else you want to share?" Danziger asked.

"Nope." Alonzo gave them a bright, hands-off smile. "Nothing else useful or informative about this place. Just that it's theirs."

"If it is a tomb, that would explain why they consider it a sacred place," Bess said. "Naturally they wouldn't want us profaning someone's grave."

"Pretty fancy grave," Morgan said, glancing around again.

"Well, Mom," Uly went on, "Yale's been making me study old civilizations, and a lot of old kings used to do this kind of thing, go off and build a gigantic tomb of some kind, fill it with his money and his furniture and all his favorite things, then try to hide it."

"That's why there are so many traps," True explained. "To keep the grave robbers away."

She gave Morgan a hard look, and he sniffed, staring right back insolently.

"At least that's what we think," Uly said. "We found out in the towers that if you don't move things, the traps don't activate. It's pretty clever."

"Yeah, but dangerous," True said. "You have to be careful."

"So we've learned," Danziger said wryly.

"But why do you think we've got the worst to face?" Devon asked them, coming back to the original point of this conversation. "It looks like we've faced just about everything they could throw at us."

"I think we're down in the bottom of the fifth tower," True said in a scared voice. "The pretty one the sunlight shines on. I think we're under the king's tomb, and if there've been all these traps before, when we were far away from him, what's going to be close to him?"

"Now, granted," Morgan said condescendingly, "this is a very pretty place, but it's a bathroom, not a tomb. You don't have any idea of where you are."

True shot him a look of pure scorn. She pointed at the opposite wall. "See those black steps?"

"What's that got to do with anything?" Morgan said. "Really, Danziger, your child gets more—"

"Shut up," Danziger said in a quiet voice.

Morgan gaped at him, then shut his mouth without a word. Bess tugged at his sleeve and whispered something to him.

Danziger walked over to the steps and stared at them. He started to touch them, and True stiffened.

"Dad!" she said.

But Danziger didn't touch. Instead he looked at Devon. "I need the scanner."

She took it to him, but True said, "It's part stone, part metal. Spooky stuff. I took its composition reading, but I didn't understand it!"

"Like an alloy," Uly said.

True frowned at him and shook her head.

Devon looked at her son. "Metals make alloys—"

"In a way, Uly's not far wrong," Danziger said, running the scanner. "This isn't quite stone, although it has various mineral properties. How strange. I never thought I'd see it way out here on a backwater planet."

Devon frowned. "What is it?"

"Don't you know?"

She shook her head.

"Orstanium. It's a space-made alloy, very difficult to create, very costly, and indestructible."

They goggled at him.

216

Devon had heard of it, but she'd never seen any. Danziger was right about its rarity and costliness. "But that's impossible. Orstanium *here*?"

He smiled. "Impossible or not, it's here."

"But how?" Bess asked.

"I doubt we'll ever know," Danziger said. "It doesn't really matter. But it does put a slightly different light on the Terrians and their past, doesn't it?"

"Nonsense," Morgan snapped. "They're primitives. They've never had technology capable of manufacturing space-age materials."

"Maybe they bought it," Uly said.

Devon looked at him in surprise. "You know, that's not a bad theory."

"Ridiculous," Morgan said.

"Why?" Devon countered. "Why shouldn't they? What makes you think we're the first advanced civilization they've ever encountered? We know almost nothing about them."

"And you still know nothing about them," Morgan said. "This is all wild imagination, nothing more."

"That's true," Bess said. "Unless we could ask them about it."

"They'll never tell you," Alonzo said softly.

"Why not?" Devon asked.

"Because it's taboo, remember? They asked us not to come in here, and we have. I think we should have to respect their privacy by not asking a lot of questions that are none of our business."

Morgan snorted, but Danziger said, "I guess he's right. Solving this mystery is less important than getting out of here. Safely and respectfully, if True's theory is correct."

Devon nodded. "Let's get to it. I don't want to delay."

The others agreed.

Danziger looked at his daughter. "Okay, True. How do we get out?"

She crossed her arms over her chest. "It's a puzzle, Dad. Everything's a puzzle here. I'm not the only one who can figure things out."

She looked tired and cranky. Devon couldn't blame her. They'd been through too much. To forestall an argument between father and daughter, Devon walked closer to the steps.

"Okay, if the kids are bowing out, it's up to us," she told Danziger.

He raised his brows and glanced back at True, who still looked defiant.

"Scared," he mouthed silently to Devon.

She lowered her gaze in agreement. "Maybe she's right to be."

The steps led to a blank wall with no evidence of a door.

Devon narrowed her gaze, uncomfortably aware of her audience. It was hard to be clever at solving a puzzle when they were all watching. But she thought she had the builders' mind-set figured out now. "No door in the wall, so there must be a door in the floor."

"Or in the ceiling," Danziger said.

She frowned. "No way—"

But just then he touched something and a panel slid open overhead. Devon climbed onto the top step and stared up at it. "Now how are we going to get up there?"

The step lurched beneath her, nearly toppling her off balance. Alarmed, then thrilled to have stumbled on the unorthodox exit, she clutched at the wall as the step rose, lifting her toward the opening. As she went up inside the opening, she saw a narrow landing with steps stretching on up into the gloom. She scrambled off, and her lift descended smoothly.

Devon peered over the edge at the faces gazing up at her. "How does it do that without machinery?"

"Counterweights," Danziger and True answered in unison.

Before she could ask anything else, the panel slid shut, isolating her from them. While Devon sat frozen, wondering if she'd entered a trap, the door opened again. She saw the step rising once more, with Alonzo and Julia on it. They stepped off beside her, and the process was repeated until everyone was up on the dark landing.

Devon shone her torch on the steps leading up into the gloom. Squaring her shoulders, she started up them. She expected to meet up with another dead end at the top, but instead she found only an open archway.

She stepped through cautiously and shone her torch around. It was a spacious area; she couldn't see the distant walls. The others joined her, and they all milled around uncertainly for a moment.

"Now which way?"

"We went down three levels originally at the temple," Devon said, thinking hard. "So we have one more level to ascend before we're out."

Alonzo switched on the solar lamp for the first time since they'd escaped the temple in the dark. At once the shadows were pushed back, but the revealed space was empty.

A little disappointed, Devon turned in a small circle, then she thought she saw either a distant reflection or a glimmer of light. She pointed, excitement quickening inside her. "That way."

Without waiting, she hurried off and they followed her. As she drew closer, however, her eager stride slowed. A huge black star of orstanium had been laid in the floor. She walked out across it without thinking, then faltered as she realized her footsteps had stopped echoing. The metal absorbed the sound rather than amplified it. She frowned uneasily. Now that she knew what it was, it seemed so wrong for this simple world, so alien.

But something even stranger lay before her.

In the exact center of the star stood a mound of sandy earth. It looked totally incongruous on that expensive metal floor, and yet she stopped, awed in a way she couldn't explain.

"What is this?" Morgan said scornfully.

Devon looked up at the ceiling. Far, far above her she could see a narrow opening.

"The top of the tower," True whispered. "And far above it, the opening to the sky. He can always be with the ground and the sky."

"And the water," Uly said, pointing.

On the other side of the earth mound stood a small basin and pedestal carved of white stone.

"The elements of the earth," Julia murmured. "Basically, that's all we are, minerals and water, fashioned in a chemical compound. In their own way, the Terrians understand this."

"Ashes to ashes," Bess whispered. "Dust to dust."

"It's just a pile of dirt," Morgan said. "Let's not bow to it."

He reached out as though to plunge his hand into the mound, but Danziger gripped his wrist and held him back.

"Don't," he said.

Morgan rolled his eyes. "Oh, come on. I'm not going to do anything to it. But let's not lose our perspective here."

"Touch nothing," True chanted softly. "Move nothing."

As though she'd dared him, Morgan wrenched free and patted the mound. He left a handprint on its surface.

Bess gasped. "Oh, Morgan, no."

"Lighten up," he said as they all stared at him in shock.

"Look, if you think I'm being disrespectful to a man who's been dead thousands of years, I'll fix it."

"You've done enough," Bess said.

But he bent over the mound and blew gently, scattering the grains of sandy loam until his handprint was erased.

"There," he said, straightening and turning around so that his ponytail swung out behind him. "All back just as it was."

In the distance, Devon heard a grating of stone, then a sharp whistle of deadly sound. She reacted instinctively, grabbing Uly and pushing him to the floor.

"Everybody down!" she cried.

They scattered, even Morgan.

A huge scythe suspended from somewhere far above swung down and across the mound, just missing it by centimeters. It swung right through where Morgan had been standing seconds before. He sprawled on the floor, gaping at it.

"Careful, it's coming back," Danziger warned.

The scythe swung back on the reverse of its pendulum, and vanished into the darkness.

They sat there, breathing hard, aware of how narrowly Morgan had escaped being split in half.

Then Danziger spoke: "Let's get out of here."

"Carefully," Devon said, glaring at Morgan. "We touch *nothing*."

"Agreed," Alonzo said fervently. "Morgan, maybe we should knock you out and carry you again. It is easier that way."

"Very funny, Solace," Morgan said. "So I made a mistake. So I'm sorry."

"So next time do as you're told," Danziger said.

Morgan glared, but he shut up.

They hurried toward the far wall but came instead to another flight of steps. These led up. Devon again took the lead, and Alonzo snapped off the solar lamp. By torchlight, Devon went up warily. These steps were very steep, and they showed their age, crumbling at the edges and making her uncertain of her footing.

There was no railing, and perhaps a meter-and-a-half of stairs separated her on either side from wide open space. She felt exposed and not too safe. Still, the steps rose to the ceiling, and hope began to fill her. The last level, she told herself.

But what guarded it? More deadly blades? A stone to fall and crush her?

She was almost afraid to put her hand on the metal panel in front of her, yet after facing the water, she knew nothing else would be quite as frightening.

She pushed on the panel, and it did not move. She pulled on it, and it swung up out of her hands, opening wide.

A horrifying stench rolled down to her, a stench of rot and death and decay. It burned her nostrils and made her flinch back.

"Ugh!"

Holding her breath and trying to pretend her eyes weren't watering from the smell, she shone her torch ahead and went up one more step.

Something came hurtling out of the dark at her, faster than thought. It hit her before she could duck, and she found her arms filled with a moldering skeleton.

She screamed, recoiling, but the thing seemed tangled up with her somehow, as though it had come to life and were trying to hug her. She screamed again, whirling around on the steps without heed for the danger of falling, and knocked the thing away.

It bounced down the steps past her, breaking apart as it did so. The skull went spinning ahead like a ball and rolled up to Julia's feet. Even she jumped aside.

"Devon!" Danziger called in alarm. "Get down——"

She turned, still shuddering, just as another skeleton came hurtling out. Devon screamed again and ducked. It slid across her back, bony fingers raking through her hair, then it was also bouncing down the stairs, shattering into fragments, the bones spinning like jackstraws.

Devon crouched where she was, her fists clenched and her eyes shut. She couldn't stop trembling.

"Devon?"

It was Danziger, hurrying up to join her. He held her close, and for a few moments she let herself cling to his solid chest.

"Oh, God," she whispered, still shaking. "Oh, God."

"There aren't any more," Danziger said, patting her shoulder soothingly. "There aren't any more."

Below, Alonzo was bending over the pair. "Guards," he guessed.

"Or architects," Morgan said. "Wasn't it the habit of the kings to kill the men who designed their tombs so no one would ever know the secret of getting in?"

"Or out," Devon whispered.

Danziger squeezed her shoulder and stood up. "Time for us to get out," he said firmly.

He went on up the steps and grunted. "Ugh, the stink."

Devon pulled herself together, aware that the others were climbing toward her now. Biting her lip and telling herself firmly that the skeletons had *not* been alive, she shook off her fright and followed Danziger, only to find that just one person at a time could fit in the space above.

"Where's the door, True?" Danziger called. "I know it's a puzzle and we should figure it out ourselves, but you already solved this one once, so give."

"Don't keep going up the steps into the tower," True said. "The door's not there. Not the real door."

223

"Okay, not up in the tower," Devon said. Her torchlight shone on the ceiling to one side of the opening where the skeletons had fallen out. "We have two doors here. One's a dead end. One's a possibility."

She tapped it and it slid open smoothly. The still, cool, musty air of the cave itself filled her nostrils, cleansing them. She inhaled deeply and boosted herself out.

The others came quickly, laughing now, moving eagerly. They scattered across the courtyard.

Bess spun around on the points of the black star, flinging out her arms. "We made it. We made it!" she cried.

Devon looked at the courtyard in wonder. It was very strange, with the individual styles of each of the five towers, the black metal star for pavement, the coral trees that glittered in their torchlight.

"It was someone's garden," Julia said, gazing around.

"An imitation of a garden," Alonzo corrected. "All the things that person down there loved."

"Placed around him," Devon said softly. She looked at Uly, feeling relief drain the tension from her shoulders. "This is indeed a wonder to see. Why did you want to keep it a secret from us?"

True and Uly glanced at each other.

Uly hung his head. "I guess we, uh, thought you'd mess it up."

"Or keeps us from coming back," True said defiantly.

"It's not a playground," Devon told them.

"No, we didn't make it one," Uly said. "Not exactly. Not like—" He looked at Morgan and compressed his lips together.

"I think we've all learned some lessons this day," Devon said. "You concentrate on what you've learned, and leave Morgan to think about what he's learned. All right?"

Uly nodded. He scuffed his toe on the ground, then

glanced up. "We, um, were going to come back before we left. We wanted to, um, well—"

"We wanted a piece of what's here," True whispered so no one but Devon could hear. "Is that wrong? Archaeologists do it all the time. Take stuff, I mean."

"I wanted to give Yale one of the scrolls," Uly said. "He's so smart he could probably decipher it, and he's never going to get to see it otherwise."

Devon smiled at him and put her hand on his head. "I'm glad you thought of him and wanted to share this with him. But I think we have to respect this place for what it is and not bother it any more than we already have."

Uly nodded. "I'll even put back the carvings I took from the fake part of the city."

She smiled in approval. "Good—"

"Devon?" Danziger called. "We have a slight problem."

Her sense of well-being vanished in an instant. Dismay sank through her. "What?" she asked. "What now?"

Danziger came striding up out of the gloom, his torch shining before him. "Believe it or not, I found a gate to this place, but it's locked."

"Locked," Devon said blankly, trying to figure out how to work this newest puzzle. "So how do we—"

He laughed, the sound worn and frazzled. "Locked," he repeated, swiping his hand through his hair. "Nothing clever or mysterious about it. Just an old-fashioned mortise-and-tenon lock worked in bronze or something. We can't climb over the wall. It's much too high."

She frowned. After all the complexities, this really was too simple to comprehend. As for what a mortise-and-tenon lock might be, she hadn't a clue. "So can't you find its frequency and—"

"Devon, it's not electronic."

"Oh." She blinked. Of course it wasn't. How stupid of

her. Sighing, Devon rubbed her face. "So how do we unlock it?"

"I don't—"

"Devon?" called an anxious voice over her gear. "Devon, are you reading me?"

"Yale?" she said, her heart light again for a moment. "Is that you?"

"Yes, indeed. I have been waiting outside these walls for quite some time in hopes of finding you. Do you require assistance?"

"Do we ever," she said. "It's good to hear your voice."

"Likewise," he replied, ever formal, but she heard more than a hint of warmth and relief in his voice. "Is Morgan all right?"

"Yes. We're all fine. A little worse for wear, but all intact."

"That is good news."

"We have a problem, though," she said.

"Yes?"

"We can't get out of here."

"I don't understand."

"The gate is locked. We can't climb out."

"I see."

"It's pretty ironic after all we've gone through," she said. "But for now we're trapped."

"Hey, Yale!" Uly broke in over the channel. "You'll never guess what we've done."

"No, indeed, I doubt that I could," Yale said warmly.

"If you brought my chair, we can fly out of here," Uly said.

There was a moment of silence. "I regret I did not think of that," Yale said. "However, I can send Zero to fetch it if you wish to wait—"

"Forget that," Morgan broke in. "Is Zero out there with you?"

"Yes, he is."

"Then it's simple. Have him break down the gates."

"No!" Devon said sharply.

Morgan scowled at her. "What does it matter? Do you want to stay here?"

"We aren't trapped. Zero can get the chair—"

"Meanwhile we could be out of here in a few minutes," he said. "Have Zero knock down the gates."

Uly tugged at her sleeve in dismay. "But, Mom," he whispered. "It won't be safe for the dead king anymore." He pointed at the ground. "You can't—"

"Yale, that's an order," Morgan said.

"Fortunately," Yale replied, "you are not my employer and I need not obey your orders. Devon?"

"No, Yale," she said, ignoring Morgan's exclamation and gesture of disgust. "We don't want to do any more damage here. Send Zero for the chair."

"Ah. I quite agree. A longer solution, but much more appropriate."

"Wait," True said. She fished something out of her pack and came forward to hand it to her father. "You told me to always be prepared, Dad. So I am."

"What's this?" Danziger asked, unrolling it. Then he started laughing.

In the torchlight Devon saw a handful of mismatched tools. "What can you do with those? The laser probes are the only thing that might—"

"No, I'm afraid not," he said. "They're the last things that would do any good."

He was still laughing. Snaking out an arm, he hugged his daughter close.

227

Alonzo frowned. "Those aren't real tools. They're just junk. How can they—"

"This old junk can pick an old-fashioned lock, that's how." Proudly, Danziger beamed down at True. "Come on, kid, let's get to work."

She grinned at him from beneath the bill of her cap. "And when we're outside, we can lock it back."

They walked away together, then True glanced back over her shoulder. "Hey, Uly," she called. "Come on, and we'll show you how."

Uly brightened and went racing off before Devon could stop him.

Julia came up to her. "Oh, that's an excellent skill for him to learn," she said, her brows raised. "When I said don't overprotect him, I didn't mean you should let him be exposed to—"

"At the moment," Devon said firmly, "picking locks is the most valuable lesson in life he may ever have. And I intend to watch."

By late afternoon they had packed up camp and loaded the vehicles. The repaired tanks were full of water, and Devon made sure no evidence of their camp remained in the cavern. While the others climbed the ledge to leave, she turned and went the other way, making one last trip to the pool of water. Cautiously she approached the edge, still feeling wary of her prophetic dream. She knew in the future she would steer clear of any more Terrian taboos. And she hoped the Terrian guardians of this place had perhaps learned that humans weren't all destructive or disrespectful. But most of all she felt she owed the Terrians something for having warned her.

"I come to say thank you," she said quietly to her reflection in the still, deep waters. "I know you don't understand what I'm saying. Maybe you can't hear me, wherever you are. But I think you can. You didn't want us to come here, but even after we defied your wishes, you gave us all the help you could. You saved our lives, and for that I'm deeply grateful."

She leaned over and brushed her fingertips across the surface of the water. Her reflection rippled and broke apart. For an instant she almost imagined she saw a Terrian face gazing back at her, then the ripples spread out and she couldn't be sure.

Thoughtfully, she stood up and brushed off her knees before going back down by the waterfall. She didn't look back at the ghost city once.

Outside, the heat struck her in the face like a blow, and the sun made her eyes squint. She put on her hat for protection and climbed into the seat of the TransRover. Her map was still in the bin. She fished it out, made a quick series of calculations, and estimated how many klicks they needed to cover today. The sun would be going down soon, making travel cooler and easier. They would have light from both moons to go by. If they pushed it just a bit, they would only have another long day of travel tomorrow and then they should find the terrain changing. They would be leaving the desert and its mysteries behind. At least for a while.

The heat felt incredibly good. The brown vista of scrub and dirt looked lovely. She smiled to herself and adjusted the mike on her headset.

"Everyone ready?" she asked. "Alonzo, any sign of buffalo coming up the valley?"

"Not so far," he reported. He had the DuneRail already stationed ten klicks southward, at the spot where they could climb out onto the western side. "No sign of them all day."

"Maybe they were just another way of guarding this place," she murmured aloud. "Natural concealment."

It didn't matter now. They were ready to go.

"Let's roll out," she said and launched the ATV down the ramp to the valley floor.

The TransRover roared behind her, slow and clumsy as it lurched down.

And far away on the eastern slope of the valley, the three Grendler watchers stood and observed their leaving. No one noticed them except Yale. No one saw them stand, with one raising its staff, except Yale. If it was a farewell, Yale kept it in his heart, to mull over with wonder.